(George)

(George)

WRITTEN AND ILLUSTRATED BY

E. L. KONIGSBURG

AN ALADDIN BOOK
Atheneum

PUBLISHED BY ATHENEUM
COPYRIGHT © 1970 BY E. L. KONIGSBURG
ALL RIGHTS RESERVED
PUBLISHED SIMULTANEOUSLY IN CANADA BY
MCCLELLAND & STEWART LTD.
MANUFACTURED IN THE UNITED STATES OF AMERICA BY
THE MURRAY PRINTING COMPANY,
FORGE VILLAGE, MASSACHUSETTS
ISBN 0-689-70409-7
FIRST ALADDIN EDITION

For Sherry Berks and Harriett Rosenberg
with love from the middle sib

(George)

before

O NLY TWO PEOPLE KNEW that George was probably the funniest little man in the whole world and that he used foul language. Howard Carr knew, and so did Howard's older brother, Benjamin Dickinson Carr. Benjamin knew because the funniest little man in the whole world lived inside of him, and Howard knew because, except for Ben, he was the only other person that George had ever spoken out loud to. For a long time. For all the years until the year of Benjamin's sixth grade when the events to be written here happened. Until then, even their mother had not known that when she gave birth to Benjamin, she had given birth to concentric twins.

But Benjamin had always known about George. He had once talked to his mother about him and told her the things that George said. Up to a certain point, Mrs. Carr had accepted George. "Most creative children have imaginary playmates," she had explained to her lady friends and to Ben's father in the years ago before he left home. "I guess that when the new baby comes, Ben will forget all about George."

Ben had watched his mother; she had told him that the new baby was inside of her and that he would come out and that that was called being born. It was perfectly logical for Ben to expect that George who lived inside of him would get born, too. But after Mother's new baby had come out as Howard and was nothing but red and screaming and couldn't talk or say any of the clever things that George did, Ben had never regretted that George didn't get born then or ever. Or ever afterwards. But Ben never mentioned George to his mother anymore. Charlotte Carr had expected George to disappear after the new baby came, and Ben allowed him to. Altogether inside.

When the new baby, Howard, was still an infant, he had cried a lot and his problem was called *colic*. As he got older, it was hard to know what to call it; but whatever it was, it couldn't be called an improvement. He didn't cry anymore; he grouched. George explained that Howard never really learned to talk; he just learned to talk back. Sometimes Ben wondered if Howard was the reason their father had left home, but Dad had gone when Howard was only two and didn't talk very much yet.

* * *

There needs to be recorded only two sets of incidents from those years before Benjamin's sixth grade. One begins at the time of Benjamin's kindergarten when Ben's special talents were discovered, and the other comes from the time of Howard's kindergarten, which reveals how Howard came to be the only other person to know about George.

When Benjamin was in kindergarten and Howard was still a cranky crawler, Mrs. Carr read to Ben an alphabet book one day. Alphabet books come in as many varieties as breakfast cereals. This one was called *Nature's Own Alphabet*. Mrs. Carr had been only the fourth person in two and a half years to check it out of the library. The pictures had come from a biology textbook. They were accurate but not pretty. This alphabet book began with *A* (they always, always do!), and so Mrs. Carr read:

> A is for Asterias,
>   The starfish of our beaches
> It has five arms with which to hug
>   Everything it reaches.

Ben asked his mother, "How can a starfish hold on to everything in the water where everything gets slippery and wet? Must have lots of teeth on its arms."

George spoke silently, "Starfish aren't really fish. They don't have teeth."

"No, it doesn't have teeth on its arms," Mrs. Carr said.

Ben insisted, "Fishes have teeth."

George said, "What did I tell you? Everything isn't what it is called. Starfish aren't fish."

"Starfish aren't really fish," Mrs. Carr said. "They have tiny suction cups," she added. Then she realized that she would have to explain what suction cups were and where they were and how they worked. So, using the picture in the book to show and tell, she explained it all to Ben. Partly because doing so was more fun than washing the breakfast dishes, which were lying under the luncheon dishes, which were also unwashed and lying in the kitchen sink.

Ben quietly listened. Ben had always been quiet; Mrs. Carr had always had the feeling that Ben had special talents and understood everything that she told him. She also knew that most mothers had that feeling about most first-born sons. When they went to the beach the following weekend, Mrs. Carr found out that her thinking about Ben may have been fond, but it was also correct.

Little Howard was sitting at the water's edge, frowning first at the sand and then at the sea when Ben picked up a starfish that had been washed ashore. It happened: He recited the poem to his mother with George silently prompting him only about the name *Asterias*. Mrs. Carr smiled, and George urged Ben to tell his mother about how the starfish used suction to walk and to open clams. George knew that it would cheer her up. Ben did, making only one error; he said something for tentacles that made

Mrs. Carr laugh out loud.

That evening Mrs. Carr had a long talk with Mr. Carr. It was the first time in months that they had discussed something with each other instead of scolding each other about it. The result of that discussion was that Ben was sent for special tests and then to Astra, a special, experimental, public school. Children came to Astra from all parts of the county, for there each student was allowed to advance at his own rate. Or rates.

There Ben was able to take English and social studies with other kids his own age at the same time he took science courses with students much older.

Ben and George had taken biology when Ben was in the fourth grade and both chemistry and physics in the fifth. George had enjoyed biology enormously, and he had helped Benjamin throughout. Joyfully he had helped. He had memorized the names of all the bones for Ben and the names of all the plant phyla like Spermatophyta and Bryophyta. He had learned the names of all the blood vessels, and he had helped Ben to spell everything correctly. In the year of Benjamin's sixth grade, two years after he had taken biology, if you asked Ben the names of the bones of the body, he would get the answers from George and tell you. There was always a pause between question and response like radio messages being beamed to the moon and bounced off so they can be returned to earth.

It was in biology that Ben had first become William's lab partner. Benjamin's reputation had preceded him into the room. He entered, and a voice called out, "Hey, Carr, come sit here." The voice had belonged to William Hazlitt, one of the most famous students at Astra. Ben had been flattered to be singled out by someone who was not only glamorous but also much older, for William was in tenth grade when Ben was in fourth. And the following year when William and Ben took two science courses, physics and general chemistry, in one year, they again were partners. Again because William saved space for Ben. Ben felt flattered but not overwhelmed.

Ben never avoided other students; he just didn't make time for them. And until the year of his sixth grade, he never seemed to need to. He was busy with school and with responsibilities at home. No one in his neighborhood went to Astra, and vacations were often spent in Norfolk, Virginia, with his father and his father's new family. Ben wandered from social studies to science and from school to bus alone. But not really. He had always George within him to amuse him and to disturb his quiet when he needed company.

It was in biology that Ben and George had learned a word that was special to them. Special and significant. *Symbiosis:* a relationship in which two things live together for the benefit of both. They had learned that lichens growing on a tree trunk are symbiotic, and bacteria growing in the roots of clover are symbiotic. *Symbiotic* is what Ben and George were. A secret symbiotic society. They wished that they didn't have to share that word with lichens and bacteria.

Whenever Ben was working out a problem, George would ask him if there was anything he wanted him to remember, any special number or other information that might clutter up Benjamin's brain. In fifth grade George had remembered all the atomic weights and all the atomic numbers of the elements and had saved Ben a lot of time and trouble during examinations. Ben could spend more time and thought on difficult problems since he always had information stored up inside of him. But George was best at solving problems that required a new way of looking at things. Sometimes it would be a zany word that George would say or sometimes just a wild point of view. Ben

(9)

and George reached for answers together. And loved it.

Ben was a happy boy. Most people who knew him didn't realize that he was until his happiness collapsed. They confused happiness with gaiety, but happiness isn't always loud and bright and crowded. Happiness ripens like a watermelon, sweet and rosy on the inside with only a thin top layer altogether free of small black pits. And, like a watermelon, the whole can be covered with a plain dark rind. Though Benjamin was wrapped in quiet, though Benjamin was shy, he was happy. George inside of him was loudmouthed enough for Ben. Ben and George got along splendidly, symbiotically, for all the years until the year of Benjamin's sixth grade when Ben's need to be accepted by others became greater than his need to be acceptable to George.

It remains to be told how Howard came to know of George.

Even when Howard was merely an infantile civil disorder, George was discovering nice things about him and telling Ben about them. "Look," he would say to make certain that Ben noticed that Howard had shared the last four Hershey kisses with him, even though the two that he gave Ben were unwrapped and wore a thin coat of lint. "Look," he would say to make certain that Ben noticed that Howard had told his best friend, Raymond, that yellow was the best color because his big brother Ben had said so. Howard began to eat ketchup on soft boiled eggs; Ben always had. Howie waved *hi* with the same snap to his wrist that Ben used. Ben had seen him practicing in front of a mirror. Howard would run up to Ben whenever he saw him and give him a firm poke in the gut and then snuggle under Ben's chin. Ben got to like the way Howard's hair smelled. Actually, Ben learned to love him. Impossible Howard. Impossible him.

The day after Howard was expelled from kindergarten was the day that Ben told him about George. Howard didn't start out being expelled; he started out being sent home. But by then Howard was the product of a broken home; his mother worked and would not be home if they sent him there; so Mrs. Hutchinson decided that even though she could not send him home, she would not keep him in the classroom any longer that day. Not for another minute. So he was banished to the playground. The Volkswagen minibus that the school used for transportation was parked on a bed of oyster shells just ouside the playground fence.

Next to loudness, Howard loved cars best. Howard's bad reputation had made the driver sit him up front right by her. All the time. To and from school. Everyday. Right up front under the watchful eye of Mrs. C. Prendergast who drove the bus. Howard, too, had a watchful eye. He watched everything that Mrs. C. Prendergast did to make the bus go. Every little thing.

Unfortunately, Howard's legs, which were long enough to allow him to climb the school playground fence, were

too short for him to get the clutch all the way down. Right after he turned on the ignition, he stripped the gears. The noise was interesting and loud, so Howard did it several times again. The fourth-going-on-fifth time brought Mrs. Hutchinson out of the classroom. She found Howard sitting in the driver's seat saying *Vroom, Vroom,* calm and happy. That was when the kindergarten expelled Howard. Howard had lifted the keys from a peg in the office on his way out. They got him for the keys, but they were really mad about the clutch.

Mrs. Carr demanded a refund of the tuition, and the school did not even suggest that they send her a check in the mail. They opened their drawer of petty cash and withdrew fifteen dollars worth of milk money, all in ones, and Mrs. Carr signed a receipt not only for her money but also for Howard. They wiped him off their books.

Mrs. Carr had to take a day off work to register Howard at the next kindergarten. The new school asked that she bring him along for the interview, and you couldn't blame them.

As she filled out the registration form, the director addressed her questions to Howard instead of to Mrs. Carr. "And how old are we now, Howie?" the lady asked.

"The big hand is on the twelve, and the little hand is on the two," Howie answered.

The lady smiled and said, "No, no. No, no. We didn't ask Howie what time it is."

And Howard replied, "And Howie didn't exactly tell you neither."

The school took Howard anyway; they specialized in kindergarten dropouts. It was very expensive and called itself "The Wee House in the Woods." Howard, however, was not certain that he wanted to continue a career in kindergarten, at least not that kindergarten. Mrs. Carr was worried that no other school would take him at such a late date and with such a reputation. She asked Ben to help her convince his brother. When they were alone, Ben began.

He opened with, "I'm sure you'll love the Wee House in the Woods . . ."

George interrupted. George doubled up just one word in the school's name and made it sound ridiculous. Ben told Howard, Howard laughed.

Howard said, "O.K., Ben, I'll go. But it's a good thing

that you thought of a good name for that dumb sissy place."

Ben told him that it was George who thought of it.

"Like George who?"

Ben told him who George was.

Howard asked, "Does he have a moustache?"

Ben answered that he didn't know because George never talked about himself, and, of course, Ben had never seen him.

Howard requested that Ben ask him now, but before Ben could, George answered all by himself, "Why would I want a moustache? They're for showing, and I never show myself."

Howard realized that the special deep voice that appeared to come from his brother Ben really came from

George. He asked Ben, "Did you swallow something special to get George inside of you?"

Ben smiled, "No, I was born special."

Howard voted to finish kindergarten on a month to month basis, and it was all understood among them after that. For years Howard, Ben, and George faced the world as Howard and Ben. Howard got along well with George; George had wanted a friend, and he found Howard a comfortable one. They looked at the world in the same way, except that Howard could see it.

After kindergarten Howard started public school. There were no special schools in Lawton Beach for his particular talents—common sense and bad manners.

Lawton Beach, washed and bleached, is the town in southeastern Florida where they all lived two years ago

when these things happened. If you think of the Florida peninsula as a swollen thumb being soaked in salt water, Lawton Beach is where you'd get a hangnail on the outside edge. The beach there is popular because it is public and because it is beautiful. Public beaches are rare in that part of Florida where tall apartment houses and hotels bead the coast and block the view. Lawton Beach has a five mile strip of public sand that butts against Highway A1A on one side and plays watch-me/wash-me with the ocean on the other.

Every spring a mighty crowd of college students storms that free beach. The whole town for Easter week becomes a carnival: loud music, swift rides on land or sea, popcorn, beer, and little sleep. It is a challenge to the local government to keep a balance between being friendly and being firm. Lawton Beach normally makes news during Easter week. It makes national back page news because youth has become a celebrity, but in that part of Florida, the college crowd creates front page news because it creates business. The Lawton Beach *Daily Sun* issues an ANNUAL SPRING INVASION issue.

If it were not for George, the events to be here recorded would have made headlines, front-page headlines, everywhere. And then some lives would have been changed forever. And for worse.

one

O<small>N THE FIRST DAY</small> of Benjamin's sixth grade, Ben ran along the terrazzo corridor, trying to slide but not slip. He was late. He had just finished physical education, and someone had tied together the shoelaces of his new shoes while he had worn his sneakers. At least new leather soles slide well on freshly polished floors; a school year at Astra always began with both and stayed smooth only as long as other beginnings do.

As he raced down the hallway, George spoke silently inside of him. "Why are you in such a hurry? Did they start a course in sex education in this place?"

"No," Ben answered silently, "organic chemistry."

"Oh, yippety do!" George exclaimed. "That's the most exciting thing you've taken since you were taken to bed with chicken pox."

"They've never had this course before," Ben explained.

"It's usually not taught until you're in college."

"I could wait."

"I want to get the same lab table we had last year. Up front," Ben said. "I'm afraid I'll be late. I hope William will get there to save us a table up front."

"Do we have to sit by him again?"

"What do you mean, have to? I hope we do. Sitting by him will make us his lab partner again. He chose me twice last year and for biology the year before . . ." Ben interrupted himself to open the door to the lab-classroom. Everyone else was already seated. William was. Right up front at the same lab table as Cheryl.

Walking into the classroom and finding everyone already seated made Benjamin feel that they all knew something that he didn't.

They did.

They knew about the chart. Ben saw it then, taped to the blackboard with masking tape. He looked at it, noticing only his name and position, the last table away from the board, and not even checking it long enough to read the name of his partner-to-be. For the first time in all his years at Astra, Ben would have to sit where he had been placed on a chart. Mr. Berkowitz had done it, and Ben had always thought that Mr. Berkowitz was liberal.

Ben hitched his books a bit higher on his hip, brushed the hair out of his eyes with his free hand, and with his eyes lowered, especially avoiding William's, he walked back to his assigned seat.

"Who is our partner?" George asked. Ben busied himself with his books and didn't answer. He often took out his mad feelings on George. George was used to it. "I know it's a girl. Smells like a girl."

At last Ben looked up and answered, "Karen."

"Is she a giggler?" George asked.

"No," Ben answered.

"I think that I'll like her better than William."

"You'd like anyone better than William. I know that you never liked him." Pause. "I liked being his partner. I was always happy when he picked me."

"He picked you only because he collects peculiarities."

"If I'm peculiar, it's you who makes me so."

"Humph! Preferring organic chemistry to sex education. Blame that one on me."

Ben smiled. The final bell rang, and the explanation for the seating chart began.

Mr. Berkowitz explained that he had set up the seating arrangement so that each of the seniors would have a senior for a partner. The seniors, he announced, would be allowed to do research.

Mr. Berkowitz had a perfect right to make such an announcement even if it did leave Ben out. Mr. Berkowitz had worked to get even that piece of a program into the school. Mr. Berkowitz was in fact the soul and spirit behind the science department at Astra. He had come to Lawton Beach a year before. Everyone then had wanted to know what would make a man with his brains and qualifications come to Florida to teach. In the course of the year they had found only two things wrong with him: He was overweight, and he came from New Jersey.

It had not been easy for a fat man from the North to convince the Board of Education that Astra ought to allow the seniors to do research. There were many reasons why the Board was worried, and one of their reasons was genuine; they were concerned about safety, and that was why Mr. Berkowitz had assigned the partnerships that he had. By insisting that the seniors always have a partner in the lab with them, he had quieted fears for their safety. He had reassured the lady who wore the flowered stretch bonnet over her hair curlers that the seniors would turn off all the lights in the lab, make certain that no faucets were dripping, and lock up before they left.

The lady in the flowered bonnet had said that there was a lot of taxpayers money going down the drain on fancy programs at Astra. Mr. Berkowitz had joked, "Lab drains never get clogged with money; it dissolves in all the acid that gets thrown down, too." The lady didn't like the joke.

Mr. Berkowitz was honest with the Board; he told them that they should not expect great and new discoveries from the seniors' research. And the School Board wondered why they should bother at all.

Mr. Berkowitz explained, "Suppose you have a child

who shows a great talent for the piano. You give him a book, and you tell him to practice—without a piano. So he reads the book and moves his fingers along the edge of a desk or a table, imagining that it is a piano. He hears the sounds in his mind, and he comes to think that he's pretty good. But is he? Can you tell? Can he? Well, I want to provide those seniors who are very talented in science with the scientific equivalent of a piano. I want to give them use of a lab. They will not be discovering new atomic particles, and they will not be winning a Nobel Prize as a result of what they do in the lab. They will not be composing new music, so to speak, but they will be learning to play some complicated pieces. They will be learning advanced laboratory techniques."

The Board wanted to hear more: It would be progressive.

More. It would help bright kids get a head start in college.

More. It would be wonderful advertisement for the community to have such a program. The Gateway to Space, Cape Kennedy, was so nearby. Wouldn't it be wonderful if people began saying that the Cape is the Gateway to Space, but Astra makes the keys to unlock the gate?

Hmmm. Very interesting, Mr. Berkowitz. More. The publicity, gentlemen, would be good for business.

The School Board voted yes—5 to 2. Five of the men on the Board were businessmen; the other was a dentist.

The lady with the flowered stretch bonnet also cast a *no* vote. She later told the dentist that Mr. Berkowitz had reminded her that Cape Kennedy was, indeed, very close by. Since it was, why wasn't he there making a lot of money instead of teaching school? Besides, she was convinced that people with moustaches were hiding something.

As soon as the first bell for the first class in organic chemistry had rung, Mr. Berkowitz explained all this to the class. There he stood looking at Ben and saying that he regretted that only the seniors could participate. There he stood, wearing a white lab coat that almost met at the third button down, and explaining to all the boys and girls whom he called young men and young women that they were the beginnings. They were the pilots. They would determine whether or not programs such as advanced courses and such as private research would work in the future. He was sorry that not everyone in the course would be allowed to do research (he looked again at Ben, most singularly looked at Ben), but if they got part one to work, if everyone helped him and the seniors to make the program a success, perhaps in future years they could get the program expanded. He asked them to make a deposit for the future.

George knew that if Ben could have wished away six years of his life, he would have done so right at that moment. He knew that Ben was longing to do research. But George was relieved that Ben would not be allowed to. Not because Ben was awkward in the lab, which he certainly was, but because George had felt neglected since Ben had gotten so involved with science. (Chemistry! Chemistry!) There had been times the year before when George had had to shout inside of Ben just to find out what the weather was like that day. And there had been other times when Ben had been working on a problem, scratching numbers and formulas on page after page of his notebook, all wound up, and George had had to fight to get Ben to put his head back and listen as they reviewed the problem together.

George was convinced that people ought to enjoy the pursuit of knowing as well as the knowing, and there he was saddled inside of Ben, who was galloping into the field of science, straight for the stable, not allowing George to smell the flowers along the way.

Besides, George was relieved that William would not be their partner. George hated people who were more concerned with appearing different than with being different. More concerned with appearing smart than being smart. William was like that. George liked people who had curiosity and insight. William had sacrificed both (if he ever had had them) for appearances and the conquest of success.

George was prepared for Ben's brooding on the way home from school; Ben would tell George and maybe

Howard of his disappointment, as if he, George, didn't already know about Ben's dreams of stirring and discovering. For the rest of that first class in organic chemistry, George said nothing that would aggravate Ben; he knew his place, and he prided himself on knowing when to keep his mouth shut.

Ben sat in the school bus, third seat from the rear, feeling gloomy and looking it. George knew Ben's mood but didn't care; he was feeling cheerful. Ben thought that he shouldn't.

"Why are you so cheerful?" Ben asked.

"I thought that as first days go, today wasn't bad at all."

"How can you say that? Aren't you mad that the seniors can do research and I can't?"

"The way I look at it, Ben, it isn't that we've lost research so much as that we've lost William for a partner."

"I never realized that you disliked him so much."

"I've kept pretty quiet about it. Wasn't that nice of me?"

"Not all that quiet, George. There were times last year. . . . Do you know what William said to me as class was dismissed? I'll tell you what he said to me. He said, 'I'm sorry, Ben, that everyone can't do research.'"

"And do you know what I say, Ben? I'll tell *you* what *I* say. I say that if everyone were allowed to do research, he wouldn't. He has as much need to be different as most people have to be honest." George was right, and strangely, wonderfully, he was right without knowing all of the facts.

William Hazlitt had begun life with a good start at being different. He appeared on earth as the only child in his family and the only grandchild on either side. He immediately got used to being an only. Later he had to devote time and energy to it, and it was sometimes difficult to be different in a school that allowed everyone to be. But William managed. At Astra where everyone wore sport shirts and casual clothes, sometimes even Bermuda shorts, William took to wearing a suit and vest and tie. Even when the temperature arched its way to eighty degrees the second thing in the Florida morning. William took karate lessons at the YMCA until two eighth graders from Astra joined the class, and then he switched to French cooking. William was a myth at Astra. He was Mercury, quick and flashy; kids called him Flash.

Because Ben had been the youngest and smallest in his science courses ever since he was old enough to read, because at first things were hard to reach, and because Ben had a natural tendency toward awkwardness, the class called him Splash. Ben didn't take his awkwardness seriously. He carried around a mental picture of himself being a scientist. As he poured from one container to another, spilling small blobs on the table top, he pictured himself pouring from one container to another, nothing spilling, and the picture labeled: LIFE MAGAZINE VISITS FAMOUS YOUNG SCIENTIST. He was always surprised when things broke or burned because to himself he didn't picture things happening that way. He thought that Splash was a funny name, but that it didn't fit him.

Ben was awkward about mixing molecules in the lab, but he was quick and graceful about pushing them around on paper. Everyone in the class regarded him as a quiet guru. They came to him for help. Coming to Ben was easier for people than going to anyone else in class because Ben was apart from them; they could afford to show him their weaknesses. Quietly Ben helped them. When they came, George would get irritated at the amount of time they took up and the little thanks they gave in return. But they never knew that while Ben was saying, "You've got to set up the proportions on the basis of their molecular weight," George was screaming, "Why don't you tell that dum-dum to run his elbow over the page? That would do him as much good as reading it does." They always thought that the smile that Ben wore as he helped them was gentleness; part of it actually was.

George allowed Ben to think these things over. Then he added, "Do you know what? I'll tell you what: Everyone knows that you're different. So William had to make your differences part of him. That's why he made you his partner."

Ben didn't answer. George was able to get in the last word, "Hunh!" he said, "Farewell, farewell. Farewell to the class odd couple: Flash and Splash."

That year, as in others, arrangements were made for Howard, whose school day was shorter than Benjamin's. It was arranged that he stay at the Sandler's and play with Raymond until Ben got off the bus, and the brothers could walk home together. Raymond was Howard's only friend and club member. Howard always had a club, not a secret symbiotic society. Once it had been a Keds Club; that was formed when Howard got a pair of Keds instead of the brand of sneakers sold at the local discount store. He told Raymond that only kids with Keds would be allowed into the club. Mrs. Sandler had just purchased for Raymond a pair of Brand X from the local discount store. Since he was not soon to wear those out or outgrow them either, Howard's Keds Club would have been without members unless he changed the membership rules.

Howard did.

He had made it the One C Club, which meant that members had to get one C on their report cards every grading period. Raymond's mother tried to break up the One C. Raymond had allowed his handwriting to become sloppy. "What do you expect to do," she asked, "change to the name to One D as soon as your handwriting gets bad enough and your grade slides right along with it?" Raymond thought that the question was one that should be answered, so he asked the President.

President Howard had replied, "Listen, Ray, we'll have to take out a new charter if we change the name to One D. You know there will be legal fees, and you already owe me $6,206 for fees and fines. Do you want to make it $6,216?"

Raymond thought a minute. "Maybe if I do happen to get a D in handwriting, I can swing it so that I can bring spelling down to a C. That would be my one C."

Howard answered, "You better just keep that C in handwriting."

And that was the thing about Howard: He knew his limits.

There were other times when Mrs. Sandler was not fond of Howard. But it was hard not to be fond of Charlotte Carr. It was hard not to want to help her out even if it meant taking care of Howard every weekday afternoon from 2:45 P.M. until Ben picked him up at 4:00. Mrs. Sandler also believed that an only child like Raymond should play with at least one other child his age. One other like Howard was *at least* and *enough* for Mrs. Sandler.

That afternoon at the beginning of Ben's sixth grade, Ben and Howard walked home from the Sandler's together, Ben dragging a heavy bookcase as well as heavy thoughts. After they walked one block, crossed the street, and turned the corner, Howard asked, "How are you today, George?"

George answered, "Exhausted."

Howard asked, "How do you think Ben feels, lugging a heavy bookcase on the outside and you on the inside?"

"I am no harder for Ben to carry around than a slight case of indigestion," George replied.

"Speaking of indigestion," Howard said, "what's for supper tonight?"

"Tonight," George answered, "our Busy Little Home-maker, known to one and all as Mother, will provide us with frozen pot pies, instant mashed potatoes, and canned peaches. The last, she calls *dessert*."

"Tell me," Howard urged, "do you eat when Ben does? Ben sure eats a lot."

"Don't get personal," George answered.

Howard appealed to Ben, "I noticed that you sure eat a lot, Ben. You eat a whole heck of a lot. Is that because you're eating for George, too? You sure eat a lot. Do you know when George eats?"

Ben moaned, "Aw, c'mon Howard. I don't pry into what goes on inside of you."

They stopped at the supermarket to buy the list of groceries that Mrs. Carr had put into Ben's lunch box along with the money for them. Benjamin and Howard were the only two people in the whole town of Lawton Beach and maybe in all of south Florida who walked to the grocery store. They were allowed to wheel their purchases home in a cart; they took turns pushing each other and the empty cart back.

After the groceries were unpacked George said, "You better get something in the oven before Betty Anti-Crocker comes home, or we won't eat until midnight. Can you imagine what she'd do to a meal at midnight? Her regular cooking is one of the black arts." Thus, George had a few words to describe Mrs. Carr in the kitchen. Few, and all of them unkind.

But even George liked it when Mrs. Carr was around. She was what she was without apology. She read good books, laughed a lot, and relied on Ben to find her nylon stockings when she misplaced them, which was often.

two

Benjamin's sixth grade was only three weeks old
when George and Benjamin had a bitter disagreement, a
preview of coming attractions. William caused it. William
who was no longer Ben's partner.

Because the organic chemistry course was special and
because its students came from many different grades, it
was difficult to arrange a schedule in which there could
be two consecutive hours for lab for everyone. Therefore,
the class was scheduled for just before lunch period. Mon-
days and Wednesdays, when they had lab work to do,
those people who were in the class gave up part of their
lunch hour. They did so willingly. All did it willingly.
Sometimes they skipped going to the cafeteria altogether
and munched on sandwiches in the lab. Doing that made
them feel devoted to their work, as Madame Curie had
been devoted, starving and stirring. It also made them feel

part of something that was intimate but bigger than themselves—close knit like astronauts, locked in together and eating on the job, sharing good times, inconveniences, and an important mission.

Sometimes someone would run into the cafeteria and stand in line to buy milk for other members of the class; no one ever bothered to remove his lab apron when he so ran. That clear plastic apron was a badge that was fun to flash occasionally. After all, astronauts telecast pictures.

Mr. Berkowitz was aware of the lack of time they had for laboratory work in class. He was also aware that a short time well spent was more useful than a long time poorly used. He stressed the importance of being prepared. Come to class knowing what you are going to do. Never lose sight of the purpose of your work; don't follow directions one step at a time. That is the way accidents happen. He summarized by urging, "Don't be a cookbook chemist."

In keeping with his policy of free enterprise, Mr. Berkowitz told the class that he would not police them. He would not quiz them on whether or not they were prepared. Instead he would watch results. Poor preparation would show up in poor results, sooner or later and more often than not. Laboratory grades, which accounted for one third of the course grade, would depend upon results. Results count in real life.

Methods of Purification was the lesson for the third

week of school. Everyone was to distill impure benzene and make it pure. Karen set up the equipment for distillation; Ben was to take it down. That was the manner in which they divided their work. Karen was very orderly even if she didn't smile very much and even if she was not nearly as much fun as William had been. George reminded Ben that he had had much more to do when William had been his partner. George was full of those kinds of reminders, and Ben only half listened. Ben wondered if George was jealous of William.

Ben was anxious to show their product to Mr. Berkowitz; their benzene was clear, just as it should be. And they had a good yield besides. Ben thought that he would like to take the benzene home and add it to his collection. It would be his first important organic chemical. He had collected unwanted products and broken equipment for two years. He kept everything in his room, all shelved and dusted and neatly labelled with Dennison stickers, which he bought in McCrory's. It gave him a feeling of order, of polish and finish, to have this tidy corner, always neat, in his mother's tumble-dry house.

Benjamin carried his flask of clear benzene to Mr. Berkowitz, who took it and held it up to the light of the window and asked, "What have we here? Ah! nectar from a cactus? Syrup from a log cabin, perhaps? Ah, no, it is indeed . . ."

"A morning specimen to be tested for diabetes," George added. But only Ben heard that. Ben laughed, and Mr.

Berkowitz was glad to see that Ben appeared happy in class again.

"Put your product into the jar labeled RECOVERED BENZENE. It's on the table in the back of the room. We'll use it again, all this good, pure benzene as a solvent for our next lab project. As the lady in the curlers would say, "Don't let that benzene go down the drain." Then Mr. Berkowitz made notes in his grade book.

Karen said to Ben, "This is one thing that you won't be able to take home." Ben shrugged; he didn't care that much. Karen always seemed borderline unfriendly. She was cool and shy, and Ben was quiet and shy, and both kept their common symptom, shyness, hidden. Thus, they faced each other as cool and quiet; they never would learn to touch.

Meanwhile, William and Cheryl had spilled half of their product over the top of the lab table. Small wonder. They had come to class late, set up hurriedly, and at clean-up time, Cheryl had knocked over their flask. While Cheryl quickly tidied up the mess, William checked to see that Mr. Berkowitz did not notice. William acted with the speed and forethought that people usually see only in practiced spies during the third season of a TV series.

William smiled at Ben as Ben stood by the corner of his lab table examining his benzene before he poured it into the RECOVERED BENZENE jar, which was just in back of where he and Karen worked. "Benjamin, my friend, would you mind if I relieved you of that heavy burden?"

(*35*)

William asked. He did not look at Karen at all, and he would not look at her throughout his negotiations.

Ben smiled at William, "I'm putting this in the recovery jar. We're not allowed to take it home, Will," he said. "I'm not taking it home."

"And neither will I, Ben," William said. He pronounced neither like nigh-ther. "I wish it only as a loan for a short length of time." Then he leaned over and whispered in Ben's ear, "Cheryl dumped ours by mistake. Can't you help your old partner out?"

Ben hesitated. Karen looked the other way. If there had been no witnesses at all, Ben would not have hesitated at all. He would have handed over the flask even before George could yell, "That's next door to cheating. Don't do it, Ben. Don't. Do. It."

"Aw, c'mon, Ben," William urged. "You don't want me to flunk and get in trouble at home, do you?" William glanced at Mr. Berkowitz and saw that he was involved with Adam and Violet up front, so he urged further. "I can't have Cheryl's mistakes pull down my mark."

"That's what partners are about, William. You're not altogether alone," Karen told him. "You're responsible for someone else, too. Like in sickness and in health."

William ignored Karen. "Just this once." He smiled at Ben. "For your old partner. For your buddy of the past couple of years who is in sickness right now."

Karen turned away again.

Ben handed William the flask.

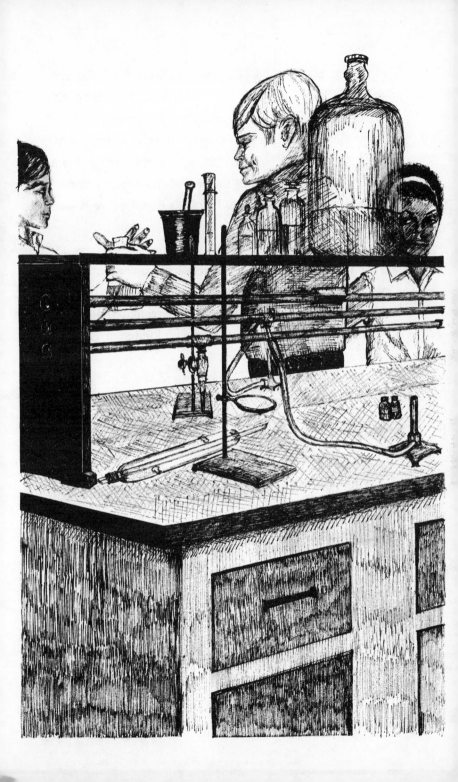

George asked, "Did you give it to him? Ben? Did you give it to him? All right. You don't have to answer me. I know. Your silence is deafening me, Benjamin. You can count me out now. I am bowing out of this organic chemistry. All those stupid sissy names: methyl, ethyl. I am going to sleep through all the rest of this organic thing."

Thus began the battle of George vs Ben. George bowed out of one part of Benjamin's life.

Ben did not do well on the first organic chemistry quiz of the year. George did not begin a sleep-in. He began a talkathon. He chanted. He sang. He recited things that he had learned for Ben beginning with kindergarten.

> *"Trochee trips from long to short;*
> *From long to long in solemn sort*
> *Slow Spondee stalks . . .*

by Calvin Coleridge."

"Don't be ridiculous," Ben corrected, "Calvin Coolidge was a president. It's something else Coleridge."

"What is it?" George asked.

"I don't know, and I don't care. I don't have time now. I've got to think."

"You never have time for poems anymore. I like poetry. Why don't you ever think about what I like anymore."

"Because I'm busy. Right now I'm very busy."

"Slow Spondee stalks; strong foot! yet . . ."

"It doesn't make any sense what you're doing to me, George."

"Makes as much sense as what you do—aiding and abetting a criminal. *—From long to long in solemn sort. . . .* Was it William Makepeace Coleridge?"

"No! That was someone else, too. Now skip it, George. I have to at least finish reading the questions."

"Makes as much sense as reading those stupid questions. All the answers are in books anyway."

"Oh, George, of course they're in books. Go to sleep, George. You said that you were going to sleep through the course. Well, prove it, George. Go to sleep." George quieted down enough for Ben to pass the test but not with the high mark he wanted and was accustomed to getting.

Next George sang during the first full-hour exam they had in Organic. He kept humming crazy commercials until Ben thought that he would lose his mind. He pleaded again with George to hush, and he did, finally, leaving Ben enough time to get through the test with nothing greater than a 78. The high mark was 93, and that was earned by Karen.

three

Soon it was thanksgiving vacation, the one school vacation that Ben and Howard were not shipped north to Norfolk to visit their dad. And they loved it for another reason besides: It was the first vacation of the school year. Early in January of each year, Charlotte Carr requested a day off the Friday following Thanksgiving. On Monday of every week she checked her November calendar to make certain that the date was still circled. That Friday was important to her; she liked to start every week thinking about it. People should have a permanently nice day to think about. Nice from either direction: From looking forward to or looking back on.

Mrs. Carr baked a twenty-five pound turkey for the three of them; she had plans for the leftovers. She also had dressing, pumpkin pie, candied sweet potatoes, and every other traditional thing, even if they came from the frozen food department, from packages of ready-mix, and from cans.

George blossomed into his sarcastic best on Thanksgiving Day. "Please tell the Queen of the Maytag that the oven will not roast the turkey unless it happens to be turned on. Tell her that the *on* button of the oven is spelled just as it is in books. O–N. I swear that if that lady, our mother, had a General Electric oven, it would get broken to corporal."

Ben told George to hush and admit that Mother was trying. But he did walk over to the oven to see if it had been turned O–N.

"Trying? Yeah, trying my patience," George answered.

They formally ate at 1:00 P.M. and nibbled informally for the rest of the day. They didn't clear the table until the evening. Mrs. Carr knew about germs, but she did not believe in them the way that Marilyn, the second Mrs. Carr, did. Marilyn was a home economics major and regularly waged anti-germ warfare. In Marilyn's house the milk cartons were put away so promptly that they never sweated, and the mayonnaise was treated like some hopelessly insane relative that was never allowed out. Ben was certain that Marilyn Carr would call the riot squad if she ever looked inside Charlotte Carr's refrigerator. Nothing was covered, and only things that made puddles were laid level.

On the Friday after Thanksgiving, Ben, Howard, and Charlotte Carr packed all the leftovers into a shopping bag and loaded them and blankets and Charlotte's chair and books and one old tennis ball into the blue Buick and drove to Lawton Beach for their annual post-Thanksgiving picnic. That picnic was always the last time they went to the beach until after Easter vacation, until after the college crowd was only a memory and a clean-up problem. The post-Thanksgiving vacation was a good tradition; it was plain, and it had grown from a real desire to do it, and it continued for the same reason. Best of all, everyone understood his part and did it and complained only enough to properly call it a *family* tradition.

The Carrs' old Buick pulled into one of the angle slots between a tan Volkswagen and a gray-green Mercury. The Buick looked like a lump of faded blue denim; it was hard to believe that it was made of metal.

The beach was crowded. There in south Florida where everyone made his living directly or indirectly from the heat of the sun, it was strange to hear how many people congratulated themselves on the weather. Fine day! they said to each other as if they had given birth to it. The sun merely did what the travel folders said that it should be doing all year long in Florida: shining. It took the Carrs at least twenty-five *fine days* before they found a spot. They staked their claim by spreading their torn, tar-stained Navy blanket that had covered acres and acres of beach for them, one square at a time. Mrs. Carr wedged herself into the half-chair that was her squat throne on her blanket kingdom by the sea. She immediately began to read.

Howard had a suggestion. "Shall I get the Cokes now, Mom, so that we can eat?"

"Not yet. Work up an appetite."

"It's worked. I've been hungry for about seven minutes already."

"We have the whole day ahead of us, Howie. If you eat everything now, you'll be hungry later, and then you'll nag me to death."

"Well, that's exactly what I'd say. Which would you rather have me do, nag now or nag later? I'm sure to be hungry both times."

Mrs. Carr did not answer. Sound doesn't travel through a vacuum. She would not answer, and she would shut him out. She bowed her head toward her book.

It didn't work.

"I peeled the carrots, so can I have one of them?"

"Swim first. You'll get cramps if you eat before swimming."

"I never believed all that stuff about cramps. I don't even believe Ben when he gives me scientific reasons about cramps."

Mrs. Carr tried a new approach. "You can eat when I begin Chapter Five. Interruptions will slow me down. I will get to Chapter Five faster if you don't interrupt me at all."

"O.K." Quiet for a minute. Howard cleared his throat.

No answer. Again. No answer. Then, "By the way, what chapter are you on now?"

Mrs. Carr held up two fingers.

"You must mean two and a half. That's not the beginning page of a chapter. The beginning page always has more margins."

Mrs. Carr said, "I am not paying any attention to you, Howard."

Howard resumed, "How many pages in each chapter?"

"I didn't even hear you ask me how many pages in each chapter."

Howard again. "Mother, there is a man with a moustache watching you."

"I am not going to look up from this book until I have reached Chapter Five."

Ben nudged Howard and whispered, "That is Mr. Berkowitz."

Howard said, "The man with the moustache is Mr. Berkowitz, Mom. Mr. Berkowitz looks like he needs something non-fattening to eat. Turkey, maybe. Turkey isn't fattening. Mr. Berkowitz looks hungry, Mom."

"If Mr. Berkowitz is hungry, that is Mrs. Berkowitz's problem."

Mr. Berkowitz, who was now standing over Mrs. Carr, answered, "The only Mrs. Berkowitz who would care is my mother, and she is living in New Jersey."

Benjamin wanted to dig himself right into the sand. There was his teacher, maker of scientists, standing there without a shirt on. There he was with all of his chest showing and showing all the hair on that chest. Pale. Pale all over except for that hair making him look more naked. It was embarrassing. And there was his mother sitting in that almost-chair, and there was his teacher looking right into the top of his mother's bathing suit. Really, thought Ben, the way she keeps growing out at the top of that suit, she ought to go on a diet. And Mr. Berkowitz with her. Mr. Berkowitz sat down right on the blanket next to Mrs. Carr and did not look at all embarrassed about how he or Mrs. Carr looked in their bathing suits or about where his eyes should go.

"For openers," Mr. Berkowitz said, "how does it feel to be the mother of such a brilliant student?"

"Getting an 82 in organic chemistry and an 86 in English on his first report doesn't make him brilliant."

"I would be frightened for him if he made high marks in everything all of the time," Mr. Berkowitz said. Then he smiled at Ben, and then he smiled at the top of Mrs. Carr's bathing suit.

Mrs. Carr looked at what he was looking at, hitched up her suit, and asked, "Would you care for something to eat, Mr. Berkowitz?"

"Sounds fine," he answered. "Just a minute; I'll be back with my things. I'm stationed a little way from here."

Mrs. Carr noticed Howard. "Close your mouth, Howard. Howard will give you a hand, Mr. Berkowitz. This is Howard."

Howard gave his mother a slit-eye look but went trotting after Mr. Berkowitz, mouth closed. Howard did know his limits.

Mr. Berkowitz returned, gave Ben money to run across the road for Cokes for everyone, and began to eat. Mr. Berkowitz was eating white meat, and Howard watched Mr. Berkowitz eating it. He chewed and looked over at Howard and then looked away. Howard didn't stop looking. Mrs. Carr offered her son potato chips. Then a drumstick. And then (even) a Baby Ruth bar, but Howard nodded no and continued to stare.

Finally, Mr. Berkowitz asked, "Why are you staring at me like that?"

"Because I don't want to miss it."

"Miss what?"

"Seeing what is proper."

"Staring isn't!" Mr. Berkowitz said.

"I am not staring at you. I am staring at what you are doing. Or *are going* to do. I have to see whether you wipe your moustache with your handkerchief or with your napkin."

"I just may shampoo it and rinse it in the Atlantic."

"Really?" Howard asked. "You know, I expect to grow one as soon as I get together enough hair. I started adding Vaseline to my upper lip every night. Someone told me that Vaseline makes hair grow. Raymond told me."

Mrs. Carr said, "So that's the trouble. I'm telling you, Howard, if it grows hair anywhere, it will be on the pil-

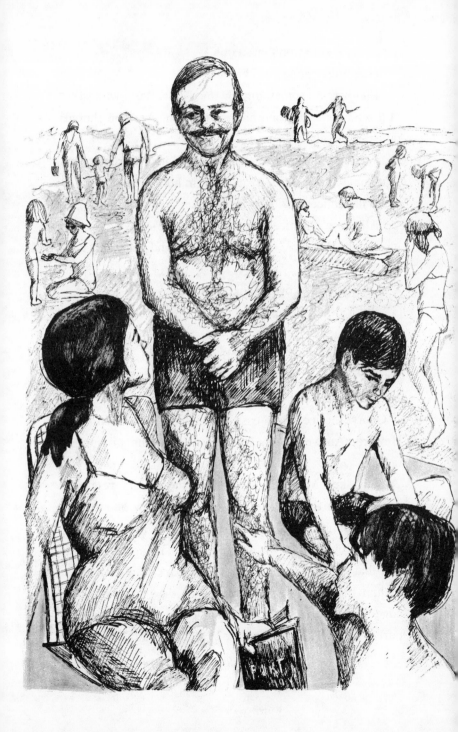

lowcases. It sure won't wash out."

"Dumb Raymond," said Howard.

"I'll give you something for that," Mr. Berkowitz said. "I'll send some acetone home with Ben. Acetone should take it right out."

"Acetone?" Mrs. Carr repeated. "I'll have to remember that name and see if Ben has some in his collection."

"What collection?" Mr. Berkowitz asked.

"All those chemicals and stuff that he's always bringing home. All those unused portions and their cracked containers."

"Oh?" Mr. Berkowitz looked puzzled.

"But I doubt if he has acetone. I seriously doubt it," Mrs. Carr added quickly.

"I doubt it, too," said Mr. Berkowitz. "I'll see to it that you get some."

"That would be very kind of you," Mrs. Carr said.

George noticed how easily Mr. Berkowitz joked with Howard. Answering back about shampooing his moustache.

Ben asked Mr. Berkowitz about the seniors' research projects—partly because he wanted to know and partly because by asking he could get a glimpse at the part of Mr. Berkowitz that the seniors were finding out about and that Howard had already talked back to. The border of him that lived slightly outside of the classroom, the edge close to friendship. Ben wanted to move in on that part of Mr. Berkowitz, because William already had.

"William used to be my partner, you know," Ben said to Mr. Berkowitz. Mr. Berkowitz nodded. "We are sort of good friends," Ben added. Mr. Berkowitz nodded again.

George was disgusted. He knew what Ben was doing. Ben was trying to make an impression; he wanted Mr. Berkowitz to be so impressed with him that he would mention him to William. Ben didn't know about friendship. George did. Friendship came naturally to George. It was always George who understood things that didn't make sense, and he knew that friendship is the most unreasonable thing in this world. A person can have a hundred reasons for not liking a guy and not a single one for liking him; he just does. Hadn't he made friends with quarrelsome Howie? But Ben thought that he had to advertise to sell his friendship.

Mr. Berkowitz, not realizing Ben's real reasons for asking, explained that William and Cheryl were to make amides, which were a particular kind of chemical the class would study later. He took a shell and wrote in the sand at the edge of the blanket, and Ben nodded yes when he understood and also when he didn't. He decided that he would look up everything he didn't know when he returned home. The last thing in the world he wanted to do was to appear stupid. He silently spoke the names of the chemicals that Mr. Berkowitz mentioned hoping that, even though they involved organic chemistry, he could count on George to help him remember what he would need to know.

But George had first friendship and then something else on his mind: Mr. Berkowitz's voice was different from the voice he used in the classroom. In class he was patient and matter-of-fact. Today he was patient and eager. Mr. Berkowitz was showing off! Not for Howard who was paying no attention and not for Ben who already knew how smart and nice he was. Not for George —certainly not for George. Mr. Berkowitz was performing for Charlotte Carr; for at the same time that George was noticing Mr. Berkowitz's voice, Ben was noticing that Mr. Berkowitz's eyes, if not his head, turned in the direction of his mother. Ben knew that she was just out of range, and that made his teacher's eyes slide ever more in her direction; something just out of reach is what *tantalizing* is.

Mrs. Carr felt those eyes, and she wanted to express interest, so she asked a question. "Is the William you are talking about, the William who has been your partner, Ben?" Mr. Berkowitz answered yes.

"Who is William's partner this year, Ben?"

"Cheryl Vanderver. She has a car and drives him to school every day."

"What kind of car?" Howard asked.

"A Mustang. A red one."

"No wonder he changed partners if being Cheryl's partner means that he gets a ride in a red Mustang every day. Sure beats the dumb school bus."

"He doesn't get a ride because he's her partner. He

gets a ride because she likes him. She comes all the way across town to pick him up."

Charlotte Carr laughed. "I wonder how his parents feel about that. They sold their old house last year and bought one in Shadowlawn, one that they could *almost* afford, so that William wouldn't have to spend an hour and fifteen minutes of each day of his senior year on the school bus. Shadowlawn is only a twenty minute bus run from Astra, and here he is getting a ride anyway."

"Yeah," said Howard. "If they hadn't moved, William would have had a longer ride in the Mustang."

"That is not the point I was trying to make," Charlotte Carr said. "But I was wrong to try to make the point that I was trying to make. So, Howard, why don't you go down to the water and build one of your giant sand-castles?"

Howard answered, "I was just going to do that anyway."

Off he went, and Ben soon joined him. Ben felt uneasy, not quite knowing why, but knowing that the feeling was familiar and happening often lately. George knew what was causing it and didn't like it. Not at all. Ben had wanted to impress Mr. Berkowitz, and he wasn't sure if he had succeeded. Ben had always felt that he, George, made him special enough, and he had never felt the need to try to impress anyone before.

Ben piled up sand for the first of his sand pillars. George knew that Ben had hoped that after a few thoughtful nods of his head, he would be able to offer Mr. Berkowitz some sharp and clever idea of his own or even catch his teacher in a slight error. *See, see clever me.* Only lately had Ben begun using his special skills to collect attention and buy friends instead of using them so that he and Ben could grow together. Ben started another turret, and Howard moved over to trim the one that Ben had just completed. Ben had to realize that he was only twelve years old and already something of a specialist. Too much of a specialist. Ben began digging the moat around the newest hump of sand that would become another castle tower. He was rushing to build one turret after another. Howard was two behind on the trim jobs. Ben was doing only his part, building more towers and building them faster and faster and never taking time to look at the whole thing. He was doing that with his life, too. And George's.

George knew that he must not permit Ben to give up having time in his life for looking at the trimmings and looking at the whole. Especially now, now at this tender age George worried about losing touch with Ben. He wanted to help Ben know things. Except for organic chemistry, hadn't he always helped? He wanted Ben to be deep in one field, but he also wanted to help Ben not-know. He wanted, oh! he wanted, Ben to think clearly about everything, especially about himself, but he also wanted to help Ben to not-know. To not-know gracefully. There were times when great truth could come from the not-knowing part. Ben had to allow room, allow time for not-knowing. But he couldn't if all he wanted was to be clever instead of real.

George thought all these things, but all he said was, "I don't give a damn about William's project."

And Ben answered, "Well, I do."

Their sand castle was enormous, elaborate and fancy; it gave a nice appearance; it made a good impression. It was polished, the work of specialists. Children and wandering adults expressed amazement. Ben and Howard listened to the praises of the people. Respect for sand castles comes cheap and lasts only as long as the tide allows. George realized then that it would take a quiet revolution to keep Ben from making a sand castle of his life, building turrets of science surrounded by moats of silence and from wanting praise and friendship instead of growth for his skills.

The tide was beginning to move in, so they returned to the Navy blanket and saw that everything was packed up, ready. Mrs. Carr and Mr. Berkowitz shook hands and said how much they had enjoyed the afternoon. They mentioned how they ought to get together again soon. Neither of them had gone into the water.

Mrs. Carr looked in the mirror after they got home. She next looked in the refrigerator, then back in the mirror and announced that she was going on a diet. Although Ben had had the same thought just a few hours earlier, he did not enjoy hearing his mother say it.

George remarked, "The Pillsbury Princess is getting programmed for romance." That, too, annoyed Ben. He didn't like having George tell him things that he didn't want to hear and that were correct.

The next evening Mr. Berkowitz appeared at the Carr home carrying a bottle of acetone. He happened to remember that he had some at home, and he happened to think why wait until Ben came back to school to get the Vaseline out of the pillowcases. He paused and added, "And I happened to think that if I gave you the acetone, you might give me a cup of coffee."

"One taste of her coffee, and he'll happen to want to soak the pillowcases in it and drink the acetone," George said.

four

THE WEEKS OF SCHOOL from Thanksgiving until Christmas are stretched thin by the pull of vacation at either end. There is the tug of *dontgetgoing, dontgetgoing* and the countertug of *finishup, finishup*. Monday of any week needs a shove towards Tuesday. Monday is no time for beginning, and yet it was on the Monday, that tug-o-war Monday, that the mysterious disappearances began. Trouble. It appeared like a pimple on the stretched skin of time between the holidays.

That Monday Ben and Karen divided their lab work as usual. Ben had finished putting all his leftover chemicals into envelopes he had brought from home: He had done his homework, had studied the lab procedure, and had known that there would be extras. William appeared at their table bringing his and Cheryl's. "Still collecting?" he asked Ben. And Ben, who thought that William was trying to make up for having taken his benzene during the distillation experiment, said yes. He had felt shy with William lately; George could have made him feel more at ease, but George wouldn't. As William presented Ben with his leftovers, he announced to the class, or at least to those who were close enough to hear, which included Mr. Berkowitz, "I hear, Ben, that if we mixed together all the chemicals in your house, threw in your brother and the kitchen sink, we'd have . . ."

". . . chemicals, a mess in the sink, and a furious little brother," George finished.

William thought that Ben laughed at him. Later Ben heard William repeating to Cheryl what he had said to Ben. William had said *a giraffe,* which was not funny. Certainly not funny enough to bother repeating, George thought.

Their equipment had been put away, their table had been wiped with the roll of paper towels they had been asked to bring from home, and Ben and Karen were checking their results when Mr. Berkowitz announced that Ron was missing his condenser. Everyone was asked to check his desk to see if by some chance the condenser was misplaced. There followed a whoosh of drawers opening and a rattle as they were searched. Then a hard clap as cupboard doors were opened, and still the condenser was missing. Everyone was mystified but convinced that it would turn up eventually. Someone thought of checking the trash containers; it was not there either.

Drawers and cupboards were closed with shrugs and without concern.

On Wednesday William missed a small spatula and Cheryl missed an entire set of beakers, sizes 400 ml to 25 ml. After that, there was never a day in that tarpaulin of time from Thanksgiving recess until Christmas that something was not missing. Something as unimportant as two test tubes, which someone might have thrown away rather than wash, or something like three-hole rubber stoppers or glass tubing that someone could possibly have miscounted. Cork stoppers and rubber tubing and Erlenmeyer flasks and a separating funnel, the only one in the whole science department. Mr. Berkowitz had lent it to Lacey, one of the seniors.

As the weeks tapered toward Christmas, the tumult in the classroom grew. At first it was just a thin wind of excited disturbance, but the climate changed. By the third week everyone felt that he was working in a thick, class-bound fog. No one wanted to take the problem to the school principal; the future of the science program should not be determined by something as unreasonable as a list of thefts. The class became anxious for vacation to begin because they all wanted to leave the problem; perhaps a break in the routine would break the chain of thefts. Mr. Berkowitz walked around the room more and more; he was monitoring. On the last Monday he discovered that an electric heater was missing from the stockroom; he announced to the class that he was going to the principal.

He looked sad and tired, and everyone wanted to help him. Almost everyone.

William suggested that they get an actual count of what was missing. He said that he knew that no one could buy his way out of trouble; but perhaps if they replaced everything that was missing by contributing some of the Christmas money that they were bound to get, they could start fresh with the new year. He announced that he had discussed the problem with his parents, and they had consented to his working in the drugstore to help pay for the equipment.

Mr. Berkowitz said that the thefts bothered him less than the idea of the thefts. It was hateful to think that his students would take advantage of the freedom that he felt they should have. He told William to make the list anyway.

So William took a clipboard and pen and approached everyone in the class and asked him to write down everything that he was missing. "Be it little or be it big, write it down," he said. Everyone did. The seniors were missing the most. Making lists is one way to get things out of your system. Which is all right if it is used to start and not to finish.

Ben and Karen were missing four test tubes and one small evaporating dish. William raised his eyebrows. Ben didn't know what to make of that, and since George could not see it, George at that moment didn't bother to make anything of it.

Messenger-Flash-William took the paper to Mr. Berkowitz and hinted that he would find it interesting. Mr. Berkowitz glanced at it, folded it, and put it in the inside pocket of his jacket. He said that he would look it over later, but he already knew what William meant.

The Carrs were just finished with supper when the doorbell rang. Mrs. Carr was sitting at the table doing the crossword puzzle, and she walked to the door carrying the paper. She looked through the small diamond-shaped window on the door, said "Omigosh," squatted down so that none of her showed out of the window and made a backwards squatting retreat calling, "Howard! Howard, answer the door." Then she stooped to pick up her shoes by the door and scooted into the bathroom and was not heard from again until she clattered out of the bathroom, made up from top to bottom—from lipstick to shoes—and said, "Why, Mr. Berkowitz, how nice to see you."

Mr. Berkowitz smiled; his teeth looked like a row of Chiclets beneath his moustache. His smile did not last. He asked Mrs. Carr if she would like to have a cup of coffee with him. In private. Mrs. Carr hesitated as she reviewed the mental picture of the congealed mess in the kitchen. She always did the crossword puzzle after supper. Mr. Berkowitz, noticing her hesitation, suggested that he would like to take her out for coffee if she wouldn't mind leaving the boys alone for about an hour.

The hour was an hour and forty-five minutes long.

Ben was pleased at Mr. Berkowitz's interest in his mother as long as he didn't have to watch it happening. George told him, though, "He's more interested in what is going on in the classroom than he is in what's going on in this house at the moment."

"You. *You* were the first one to say that Mother was interested in Mr. Berkowitz as a date."

"I was the first one to say it, but we were both the first ones to think it. Together, Ben, we thought it. But tonight your mother and Mr. Berkowitz have different reasons for wanting coffee."

"He likes her. I can tell. And if you were honest about it, you would tell, too."

"Benjamin Body, I am never anything but honest; you don't always choose to recognize that, but I am honest, and really rather charming. You don't always choose to recognize that either. But right now, I would say that Mr. Berkowitz is discussing with your mother all those thefts in the lab. He likes our Chef Burn-Ar-Dee all right, but he likes order in the classroom also."

"Are you talking about the lab? About those thefts in the lab?"

"The lab. The organic chemistry class; it's all the same. I haven't noticed you skating me down the hallway to go from one to the other. Yes, I am talking about the thefts in your lab."

"What do you know about them that I don't?"

"I know, dear Benjamin, that you are Prime Suspect One. And that Karen is suspect one prime."

"How come you know that?"

"Because I'm here and you're there, and I don't get confused by a lot of outside happenings. I can come to conclusions faster than you can."

George was right.

Mr. Berkowitz did not stay long after he brought Mrs. Carr home, and she sent Howard to bed right after that. She wanted to talk to Ben alone. They went into the kitchen and as they talked, they cleared up the storm damage, which is what George always called the aftermath of one of Mrs. Carr's meals. Mrs. Carr was washing dishes as she asked, "Is there anything you want to tell me, Ben?"

"I told you so. I told you so," George chanted inside of Ben.

"If you mean all that equipment that is missing from the chem lab, Mom, I had nothing to do with it."

"I didn't even mention the lab equipment, Ben. What makes you bring that up first thing?"

"Listen, Mom, with Mr. Berkowitz coming over and all that has been going on in class and that list being passed around today, it doesn't take a powerful brain to figure that out."

George said, "Humphf."

Mrs. Carr said, "That's true, I guess. Anyone could

have figured that out."

"But not as fast," said George. "You know that without me, Ben, you'd be only half as smart as you are."

"Anyone only one-fourth as smart as me could have figured that out," Ben said to his mother (and to George).

Mrs. Carr continued. She spoke slowly. "You have that whole big collection of stuff in your room, Ben. We mentioned it to Mr. B. during our post-Thanksgiving picnic, remember? You know, I felt that I didn't want to show it to him. I think that it would be hard for someone to believe that everything in there was leftover from class this year."

"It wasn't. I saved stuff last year and the year before, too. Chipped test tubes and odds and ends of glass tubing. You don't doubt me, do you, Mom?"

"I believe in you, Ben."

"But do you believe me? Believing in me means that you think that if I took the stuff from the lab, I had a good reason for doing it. Believing me means that you know that I didn't do it at all if I tell you that I didn't do it at all. I need to feel that you do both—believe me and believe in me."

"Sometimes, Ben, we do things that we aren't completely in charge of. Sometimes, Ben, our inner self is a very different person from our outer self, and the one loses contact with the other and acts irresponsibly."

"I am on excellent speaking terms with my inner self, Mother. I didn't take the lab equipment, and my inner

self didn't tell me to do it without letting me know about it. Now, do you believe me?"

"Yes. But a little too late. Ben, I got carried away by seeing that list. You and Karen were missing just enough. Just enough to try to throw suspicion off. Karen swore that she took nothing but said that she wasn't sure about you. And Mr. Berkowitz wondered if you resented not being allowed to do research. He was really concerned about you, Ben. I respect him so much. I was too ready to jump to conclusions." Mrs. Carr pulled Ben toward her. "I told him that I would talk to you about stopping all this." Ben stiffened. Mrs. Carr continued, "I told him that I was certain that if you were responsible for all the trouble in the lab, that if you were unconsciously stealing, I was sure that you could bring those urges under control. Ben, I told him that without talking to you." Mrs. Carr shook her head, dropped her hands from Ben's shoulders, and said softly, "I sure get a D minus in motherhood today."

Ben said nothing.

George was outraged. "Of all the nasty things to accuse me of. Making you steal! That was downright nasty of her. Nasty. Rotten. The most irresponsible thing I ever did was to let you sleep in two days last year. That was the worst damn thing. And you had that cold, anyway. And also anyway, it wouldn't hurt her to be the first one up for a change."

Ben did not answer his mother or George. He was too

disappointed in the one to even mention her name to the other. Besides, George wouldn't shut up long enough to hear what Ben might have to say. Mr. Berkowitz and his mother both thought he would steal from his beloved chemistry lab. William probably thought so, too. And Karen.

The thieving stopped.

Nothing at all was missed on Thursday, the day after Mr. Berkowitz spoke to Ben's mother. That day Mr. Berkowitz announced to the class that he would place a carton in the corner of the stockroom. The person or persons who had taken the equipment could return the pieces to that box and no questions would be asked. If enough equipment was returned to show good faith, nothing would get reported to the school principal, and the seniors would be allowed to continue their research over vacation. Everyone but Ben acted delighted. William did and Cheryl did and Ron and Lacey and Adam and Violet. Even Karen.

Karen said to Ben, "Did Mr. Berkowitz talk to you personally about the missing equipment a couple of days ago?"

"No," Ben answered. "He went to my mother."

"He called me out of English class the day that William passed that list around. It seems that we were the two who looked most suspicious."

"You could have saved him a trip to my house." Ben

looked hard at Karen. "Why didn't you, Karen? Why didn't you tell him that I didn't take anything that wasn't given to me? Leftovers and chipped test tubes are all I took."

"I told Mr. Berkowitz what I saw. That I never saw you take anything, just as you never saw me take anything, but how should I know what I can't see?"

"The same way that I know things that I don't see, Karen. The same way."

George said, "Hold it, Ben. Hold it! She may not have a George to help her out."

Karen said, "You gave the benzene to William when you shouldn't have. You can't always be sure about people, Ben."

"I thought that you would understand. It's too bad you feel that way, Karen."

"I guess it is. But it's something that I'll always have with me, I think. I don't expect anyone to ever stick up for me."

George said to Ben, "You see, Ben, what happens when you trust only what you see!"

Ben said nothing.

Karen began walking away, but she turned around and added, "I'm sorry. Sorry that I didn't reassure Mr. Berkowitz harder." She paused and smiled, more to herself than at Ben, and added, "You know, Ben, even as I said that I was sorry that I didn't reassure Mr. Berkowitz harder, I was saying it because I felt that I owed it to you to say it. I wasn't saying it because I really am sorry for not believing in your innocence." She turned again to go, but hesitated and without looking around said, "And for that I am sorry, Ben."

The only time that Ben's feelings sank lower that week was the next day when he passed the stockroom on his way to the cafeteria. He glanced into the box and noticed that a dozen test tubes and some Erlenmeyer flasks and the set of beakers, sizes 400 ml to 25 ml and about three yards of rubber tubing had been returned. Everyone in the world had had a chance to return them there. Including Benjamin Dickinson Carr.

On that last day of school Ben carried his lunch tray over to where William was eating with Cheryl. Adam and Lacey, and Ron and Violet were still waiting in line to be served. Ben would never have had the courage to sit down in the midst of six seniors.

Cheryl and William smiled at him. "I saw Berky for only a minute after class; he said that the research will continue," William volunteered. "Thanks for helping out, Ben."

"That's all right," Ben said, not for any reason except that whenever people thanked him, he automatically said that. Ben started to explain that he really shouldn't be thanked when William changed the subject. "Going to Virginia to see the old man over Christmas, Ben?" Then William turned to Cheryl and explained, "Ben's daddy lives in Norfolk, and Ben and his brother visit him every Christmas. What's your father's new wife's name?"

"Her name is Marilyn," Ben said. Ben noticed that Ron, Vi, Adam and Lacey sat down three tables away, and Ben felt that he was the reason. Why else didn't they come sit with William as they usually did? "I hope I didn't take anyone's seat," he said.

"Oh, that's all right," Cheryl answered.

Ben thought that since he was taking up their time, he ought to be entertaining or helpful or something.

"I think that your research is the most difficult one of all. Making amides can be tricky."

William and Cheryl smiled at each other.

"I'm sure glad that all those thefts stopped so that you can go on."

"We're glad, too," Cheryl said. She and William smiled at each other again but said nothing.

Ben said, "Now you won't have to take that job in the drugstore, Will."

"Oh, I think I'll do that anyway. I applied and was accepted already. I guess I want to."

Ben said, "I'm relieved that you're doing it because you want to. It would make me sad to think that you were doing it just to get someone out of trouble."

William smiled at Cheryl. "We know how you feel, don't we?" Then he looked at Ben and said, "We understand all about it, Ben."

"I really want you guys to do research. Really I do."

(*68*)

"Sure you do, Ben. Sure you do," William said.

"I have a theory about those thefts."

"So do we, Ben. So do we. Everyone is entitled to a theory. After all, if Einstein and Newton were entitled, why shouldn't you be?" William laughed.

"Don't you want to hear my theory?" Ben asked. George was getting ill; he said, "They're going to say *no*, Ben, and then what are you going to do?"

Cheryl smiled at Ben and said, "Some other time, huh?"

George asked, "What are you going to do now?"

Ben didn't answer George. Since being helpful didn't work, maybe being entertaining would; he tried a joke. "Did you hear about the sick molecule?"

William said, "No, tell us about it."

"It had *a tomic* ache." Ben laughed.

Cheryl and William moaned together. George did, too. George moaned automatically upon hearing a pun.

William said, "Hey, Cheryl, I have to stop at my locker before the next class." Then he turned to Ben and said, "I hope that you'll excuse us, Ben." He and Cheryl left.

George told Ben, "That was the most disgusting performance I have ever seen. I would say that it was vulgar."

"I don't think it's vulgar to be friendly," Ben replied.

"Buttering up William as if he were an English muffin."

"What is wrong with a guy wanting a friend?"

"There's nothing wrong with a guy wanting a friend.

Heaven knows, I wanted Howard for a friend, but there is something wrong with grovelling for one."

"What's grovelling?"

"What you just did." And George had it in for William more and yet more because he had humbled Ben.

five

ASTRA'S CHRISTMAS RECESS began. There was a gap of only one day, a Saturday, between the end of school and the time Ben and Howard boarded the plane to go to their father's house in Norfolk. Ben was full of George's complaining and swearing. Howard was full of Dramamine. Dramamine had two advantages; it kept Howard from throwing up, and it kept him sleepy. Ben felt that he could not handle a restless Howard as well as a restless George.

Ben and Howard visited their father and his new family during Christmas, during Easter, and for one month during the summer, but they didn't much care for it. It was in the contract under visiting privileges. They called their father's new wife *Marilyn* even though she would have preferred that they attach something like *Aunt* or *Cousin* to the front of it. She had once suggested *Auntie*. Howard had refused; he had to call people ma'am and sir often enough when he didn't mean it. People in the South do. So he decided right from the beginning, right from the first time they met, that he would call his father's wife just what she was and what she was to him. Marilyn. Nothing more. Nothing less.

Mr. Carr's new marriage had resulted in one daughter instead of two sons. Their half sister was named Frederica, which is the only polite thing that Howard ever called her. When his mother had told him that on his next visit to his father's he would see Frederica, he had thought he was going to see a town. He still thought that his half-sister sounded like a town.

He didn't appreciate all the fuss that was made over her either. "Boy," he had complained to Ben, "they make more fuss over my half-sister spitting up clotted milk than they do over the fact that I've learned to read. Half-sister. They sure don't treat her like half of anything. She gets *all* of everything."

George said, "She's half size, half bald, and half wet, top or bottom, all the time. That makes her half." And Howard remembering that, allowed himself to endure the fuss that everyone made over Frederica Carr.

Ben looked forward to his visits to his father's house with a mixture of longing and loathing. He kept meeting the pits inside his happiness watermelon. He always had the feeling of wanting to be at his tiptoe best when he saw his dad. He wanted to show his father how much he had grown, how much he had improved, for Ben was nagged by the suspicion that if he had been a truly terrific fellow, his father would never have left. Ben was anxious to show his father just what he was missing by choosing to live with another wife in Norfolk, Virginia. The days before a visit to his father were filled with fantasies about how he would look to his dad, and the days following were filled with wondering if he had been a success.

Ben did enjoy the comfort and order of Marilyn's. George called Marilyn, *Mrs. Nasty Neat.* He knew that the chemist in Ben admired straightened drawers and closets. Ben never directly told his mother how Marilyn was; he hinted a lot, and she knew that he wouldn't mind if she improved in a direction toward Marilyn.

Mrs. Carr had packed the Christmas present that she had bought for Frederica. Freddie was surrounded by toy lessons. Putting round pegs in round holes or stacking plastic doughnuts on a peg with the smallest one on top. Frederica neither stacked nor put; she sucked. On everything. And then scattered it over the floor. Marilyn was teaching her pick-up. Howard complained because Marilyn had everything turned around. All of Freddie's toys were for education instead of for fun, and all of her education was for fun. Like learning pick-up was supposed to be fun.

So Howard had suggested that Mrs. Carr buy Frederica a gun, and Mrs. Carr had said that girls don't play with guns, and Howard had said, "Who said *play*?" Mrs. Carr smiled to herself; she would have been less than human if she had not been secretly pleased that her boys preferred her to Marilyn and almost always preferred their own tossed salad home to Marilyn's tomato aspic one. She bought Frederica blue jeans with ruffles.

Ben and Howard had received their gifts from their mother on the Saturday before they left. Once during a conversation between them, in which they tried naming the advantages of having divorced parents, they had put celebrating two Christmases at the top of the list. It was also the only entry on the list. In all the years that they had been shipped to their father's for this holiday, they never once thought about how it might be for their mother left at home alone. And Charlotte Carr never told them, but she hugged them special every year as she put them on the plane. Ben was always too full of airline schedules and Howard too full of Dramamine to notice. But George did.

This year Ben showed relief as he zipped the fuzzy lining into his raincoat and put it on. Insulation. Insulation not only from the cold they would find in Norfolk but also from the sun, steam, and laboratory routine of Lawton Beach. For once Ben wanted to forget chemistry. He would try to forget it at his father's.

But George would not let him. George, who hated organic chemistry, would not let Ben turn it off. He nagged. He began immediately after they arrived, and he continued whenever they had a quiet moment. In the car as

Marilyn drove them to the home of her mother and father. Sitting at the table waiting to be served Christmas dinner. Any little niche of time, George nagged about the lab. But he was his worst at night. Then he never let up. George was like a night fever. He was furious. He had been blamed by Mrs. Carr and Mr. Berkowitz, and he was suspected by Karen.

Two days after Christmas, George's fury reached a climax. He was determined to get to the heart of the matter. Howard had long since fallen asleep, and Freddie had had her night-night kisses, which Howard claimed were bearable only if you kept Kleenex handy. George began grumbling.

Ben pleaded, "All year you have been telling me to relax about not-knowing, and now you are begging me to pick a certain situation apart and examine it for flaws. I don't see what that has to do with me. The case has been closed, and I know that I'm not guilty."

"Stupid. It's *me* they're blaming. You've got to clear these things up. Besides, I think that what happened in the lab is only a symptom, the way that pimples are a symptom of chicken pox, but a virus is the reason you get the pimples. There's a virus named William behind all this."

"You can be brutal, George. You are really very unkind."

"I am kind to kindness and lovable to lovableness and . . ."

"And conceited."

"And also absolutely uncanny about sensing when things don't fit. To begin with, why didn't the separating funnel or the condenser show up in that carton? They are being used for something. Why are they needed?"

"I don't know, George. I'm sleepy."

"And what about the electric heater? It should have been returned. It was more valuable than the set of beakers that was. And so was the condenser and so was the separating funnel. Who was missing that set of beakers?"

"I don't remember, George."

"I do. It was Cheryl. She probably had them hidden. Some of the stuff was taken just as a cover-up for the stuff that was needed."

"Aren't you being as unfair to Cheryl as Mother was to you?"

"Maybe. But I'm keeping it to myself. I'm not making an out-loud accusation."

"That's what you think. You've been talking out loud without realizing it."

"Never mind. Howard is asleep anyway. What is William's project?"

"I don't remember. Goodnight, George."

"Don't lie to me, Ben. This is George you're talking to."

"So what if I do remember? I also remember that day at the beach when you told me that you didn't give a darn about William's project."

"I did not say that I didn't give a darn; I said that I didn't give a damn. That was because you were interested only to impress Mr. Berkowitz and because you were annoyed that there was something in this organic chemistry world that someone knew and that you didn't know. Now tell me."

"They are supposed to make amides out of compounds that have an indole ring. Can I go to sleep now?"

"Amides? What are amides?"

"They are a certain kind of organic compound. If you hadn't decided to cop out on organic chemistry, you would know that. According to Mr. Berkowitz, they are supposed to be making amides out of compounds that have an indole ring."

"Don't think that you are going to put me off by using those big names, Ben."

"I have to think about them with the words that I have for them. How else can I think about them? What do you want me to do? Think of making amides with words like mashed potatoes and succotash? Do you like those words better? You really don't have much respect for chemistry, do you, George?"

"Let us say that I feel that I must save you from being just a chemist."

"Save me from being a chemist? That's what I want to be!"

"That's the second time you've quoted me incorrectly. I am going to save you from being *just* a chemist. Which means being *merely* a chemist. Weren't you listening before?

"I'm sleepy, George."

"Foggy brained is what you are. I intend to see that you are not just a neat, prepackaged chemist who fits things into neat, labeled jars. And everything that doesn't fit into ready-labeled jars is placed into a jar anyway and put away until some label can be put on it. Chemistry is all formulas and boundaries, and I, I, me, nasty, vulgar George, intend to keep you slightly out of bounds so that you can move, swing. In short, Benjamin Body, I intend to make a man of you, a man that I'll be proud to live in. And you can shut your mind to all the messiness in the lab, all the stealing and all the funny goings on because you are afraid of making waves, making someone not like you because of what you may stir up. You don't want to care because—Ben. Ben. Ben, are you sleeping?"

"No, George, thinking."

"Good! In the morning I want you to sit down with pencil and paper and think about William's amides. I want you to think until you can make indole ones and findole ones and Dole pineapple ones . . ."

"I have to do some research first. Book research, George. I'll need some of my reference books at home. Can I be on vacation until I get home? Then I promise that I'll investigate William's project from beginning to end."

"Well, Ben . . ."

"I'm promising you that I'll do it, George. But not now."

"I'm afraid that my time with you will run out, Ben."

"All I want to do is sleep. Will you let me sleep late, George? Will you let me at least do that?"

"That's against my principles."

"I don't ask you very often. Only twice last year when I had that cold."

And that was true, so George agreed. Had he known what awaited their awakening, he would have allowed Ben to sleep even past noon.

When Ben came down to breakfast at ten-thirty in the morning, he said to Marilyn, "Boy, it sure feels good to be the last one up instead of the first one."

Marilyn smiled the smile of the detergent lady who knows that her whites are whiter and replied, "Doesn't your mother get up and start the coffee?"

Ben began, "Well, hardly . . ."

And George screamed inside of Ben, "She's looking for a halo, Ben. Don't make our mother look like Queen Frozen Pot Pie."

Ben listened to George and told his father's wife, "I have what you might call a built-in alarm, so I get everyone up in our family."

Marilyn said, "Oh, Big Ben, eh?"

Ben answered with a smile, not at her remark, but at the voice inside of him that added, "No, Little George."

Marilyn turned her back on Ben and began cutting and squeezing oranges, rich in vitamin C. Charlotte Carr who lived in Florida three houses away from the nearest orange tree didn't own an orange juice squeezer. For years her boys had thought that oranges were for eating only, and orange juice came in cans like any other respectable juice. Frozen. In cans. And on special every fourth Tuesday at the Qwik-Chek near their home. Marilyn whooshed out an orange and as she lifted the hollowed out peel from the squeezer, she looked out the kitchen window at Howard and Frederica getting Good Fresh Air and Exercise in the backyard. Marilyn began, hesitantly at first. "Ben, I let you sleep in especially late today for a reason." Long pause. Significant long pause. "I let you sleep late because you needed the rest. You've been very restless at night." Marilyn turned toward Ben and asked, "Have you been having nightmares?"

"If I have been, Marilyn, I don't remember them," Ben answered.

"Well, you've been talking in your sleep so much, Ben. In two different voices. Like a lawyer conducting an investigation."

"Uh-oh," George moaned.

"I pointed it out to your father, Ben. Last night we both listened. And I have an important question to ask you, Ben." Long pause. Concentrated removal of orange pits from cut half of orange she is holding. "Do you feel persecuted, Ben? You know, picked on? Back in Lawton

Beach, I mean. Do you feel that everyone back there is against you?"

"No."

"*I'm* not sure about that, Ben. Let me put it this way. In all those science courses that you take. Those accelerated courses that you take at Astra, have you ever had any psychology?"

"No."

"Well, I have, Ben. When I was in college studying to be a teacher, I took all the psychology courses that I had to in order to be able to teach."

"I thought that you took home economics."

"I did, Ben. But I had to have some courses to help me understand *who* I would be teaching."

"Didn't you know that you would be teaching kids?"

"Yes. Yes, of course, I knew that I would be teaching children. Girls. But I had to know what makes them do the things they do. So I took psychology courses. I loved those psych courses. We used to call psychology courses, psych courses. And political science was poly sci. I loved my psych courses, Ben, and I took a lot of extra ones. As a matter of fact, I ended up with a minor in psych. Psychology."

"I didn't know that about you, Marilyn," Ben said.

"Well, it's true. And sometimes, Ben, it's not good to know as much about children as I do. From my minor in psych and all, I mean. I know almost too much about children."

"You sure run a neat house, though, Marilyn. The Home Ec must have taught you something. And Frederica is neat, too. The dry parts are. Why do you say you know too much about children? Do you think you give Freddie too many educational toys?"

"Heavens, no. Not that."

"Why do you say that then, Marilyn?"

"Because sometimes I see things that other people, people very close to other people, never pay any attention to."

"Yeah, like Madame Curie noticing that as the amount of pitchblende got smaller, the glow got brighter. That was because the radium was purer."

"It's not *quite* like Madame Curie, Ben."

"Well, what's psych got to do with my nightmares, Marilyn?"

"But you said that they weren't nightmares. And that's what has gotten me worried, Ben."

"Why worried, Marilyn?"

"Because it just came to me, Ben, last night as your dad and I listened, that you are a classic example. An absolutely classic example."

"Why would that worry you, Marilyn?"

"Because of what you're a classic example of, Ben."

"What would that be, Marilyn? What am I?"

"A schizophrenic, Ben. A paranoid schizophrenic." Marilyn looked at Ben. No reaction. "Do you know what that means, Ben?"

And George answered inside of him, "It means that I want to get the hell out of here."

Ben said, "I don't know what it means, but it sure doesn't sound like anything nice to tell someone that you practically live with. On holidays and summer vacations."

"But I think that you can be helped, with professional assistance. I've discussed this with your father, and after listening outside your room, he's convinced that I'm right. I want you to know, Ben, that it wasn't easy convincing your father that you're crazy. He is still your father and feels very warm towards you. But I persisted, and finally, he agreed."

"Is that what paranoid how-do-you-call-it means? Crazy?"

"Well, that's a bad choice of words. I wouldn't say *crazy* . . ."

"But you did say it," Ben reminded.

"Let's not argue, Ben. Let me explain. Paranoid schizophrenic means that you have a split personality. That actually you have two personalities, Ben, and that part of you, one of your personalities is totally out of touch with reality, out of touch with what is happening. And that part talks in a deep voice and believes that everyone in the world is in a plot to get the other part."

"Not everyone, Marilyn."

Marilyn closed her eyes and slowly waved her head back and forth. "With help and understanding, Ben, I believe that we can see you through this. Your father got in touch with your mother this morning. She has contacted a psychiatrist who has been recommended to us by Frederica's doctor. It was all arranged this morning while you were sleeping in. They were roommates in college, the psychiatrist and Frederica's doctor."

"What does one doctor's knowing Frederica have to do with another one's knowing me?"

"Obviously, we don't want to send you to a perfect stranger."

"But he is a perfect stranger. To you and to me," Ben persisted.

"You see, Ben, you're arguing." She shook her head. Ben shrugged. "We're sending you home so that you can begin your therapy. You'll begin therapy right away. Therapy is what they call treatment for mental disorders."

"I've heard that word before, Marilyn."

"Yes," Marilyn smiled. "You are a bright boy. And I want you to know, Ben, that your father and I will be in communication with your psychiatrist at regular intervals, and that anytime you feel the need to discuss your troubles with us, we will be no farther away than the nearest telephone."

"Her and the friendly finance company," said George.

"You can reverse the charges," she said. Ben was silent. "I know that this is all something of a surprise to you, Ben. Finding out that you are going home and that you are a schizo when you weren't expecting that either. Schizo is what we called schizophrenic in psych. We are so very

(*85*)

concerned. So very concerned, your dad and I, that we don't think that there's a moment to lose. And we think it will be better for you and for Frederica."

"Is it contagious?"

"No, Ben, but we want Frederica to experience only the most normal things. We don't think that it is fair to her to expose her to having to make compromises with her normal growth pattern."

"I get it," said Ben.

Marilyn was looking at Ben with her head slightly tilted and her mouth slightly smiling. And the whole look had been only slightly rehearsed.

"I understand," Ben muttered. "I'll go up and pack."

Ben turned to go, and George said, out loud and in the public of Marilyn, "Marilyn, old girl, you are possibly the world's greatest jackass."

And when Marilyn heard George's deep, dark insult pour from her stepson's lips, she again slowly waved her head and said, "Poor fella."

six

THE BUICK, MR. BERKOWITZ, AND MRS. CARR were waiting for them at the airport. In years past Mrs. Carr had met them at the airport all corseted and nylon hosed, ready to take them out to eat as their coming-home treat. This year she was dressed much the same as she had been in years past, but her face looked as it did when one of them had a sore throat or was coming down with one.

She smiled at them together and then at Ben alone, and her smile broadened. She shrugged her shoulders, reached over and hugged her Ben; right there in public, at the airport terminal in front of Mr. Berkowitz, she hugged him.

And then she said, "You know, Ben, I think that Marilyn is just possibly the world's most terrific jackass." She said that. Right there in the airport terminal in front of Mr. Berkowitz and any one else who cared to listen. She tipped Ben's chin toward her and said, "We have to see this through, Ben."

"Why?"

"Because if they find out that you are not psychologically sound, and they can show that living with me is harming you emotionally or any way, they may request that you live with your father and Marilyn instead of me."

"Who is they?" Ben asked.

"The court. The judge. The divorce court."

Mr. Berkowitz looked awkward. It is very difficult for a heavyset man to look unwrinkled or unruffled. He put his hand on Ben's shoulder and said, "Well, Ben." He cleared his throat and said, "Well, Ben." Ben looked puzzled, and Mr. Berkowitz added, "Well, Ben, it's good to have you home."

Howard asked, "Would I have to go, too, Mom? To live with Marilyn?"

"If Marilyn and your father sued for custody of you; that is, only if they asked for you."

"He's safe," Mr. Berkowitz said and gave Howard a light clip under the chin.

The others laughed, and then as if a spell had been broken, Mr. Berkowitz swung into action. He announced that he was taking them all out to supper. He had invited only Charlotte Carr, but when she had to change her plans to include a trip to the airport, Mr. Berkowitz had changed his, too. He was on vacation after all, and in the morning he would be leaving for New Jersey to visit his mother. He carried the luggage from the terminal, put it down in back of the car, and after only three tries with the key, got the trunk open. Mr. Berkowitz seemed much less awkward when he was in motion. For example, when Mr. Berkowitz returned them all home and after the trunk was emptied, and all he was doing was standing close, very close to Mrs. Carr and telling her good-bye and all she was doing was standing close, very close to him and wishing him a pleasant, safe trip and all Howard and Ben were doing was watching, he appeared awkward again.

Ben's first appointment with the psychiatrist was for 10:00 A.M. the next morning. Mrs. Carr was taking the day off work to get him there. George told Ben that he would get him up in plenty of time.

"I'm glad that I can count on you for that at least."

"I would like to know what you *can't* count on me for, Benjamin."

"I can't count on you to be quiet."

"And I can't count on you to tell me when Marilyn is listening at the keyhole."

"This may come as a complete shock to you, George, but I cannot, repeat, cannot see through doors. And I can't hear sounds that aren't made. Like Marilyn didn't make any. Does that throw you, George? To know that I can't do those things?"

"No, Benjamin Body, that information does not throw me. Because I am often surprised that you can see what is there. Your bumping into things in the lab is a legend in its own time. There is much to be seen that is outside a test tube, and there is much to be heard when people talk besides *what* they say."

"George, you are talking out loud again. What is the matter with you? I never had to tell you before when to do your talking silently. You always knew. It was always understood between us."

"I had to talk loud at Marilyn's to keep you awake. You were hung up on getting some sleep. Sleeping your way out of a problem is what you were trying to do."

"Hung up? Hung up on getting some sleep? I was plain tired. Tired of your nagging. You were hung up. Hung up, nothing. You were crazy on the subject of the thefts in the lab. What are you trying to be? Sherlock George Holmes and James George Bond all rolled into one, and, unfortunately, all rolled into me? Do you know what I think? I think that you're the one who is crazy, George. Not me."

"*Unfortunately,* rolled into you? Is that the way you feel about me, Ben? Is that the way, after all these years?"

"You have gotten so loud. So loud, George. See. See. You're talking out loud again. Shouting. What is happening to you? Are you losing control of yourself altogether?"

"No, I'm not losing control. What I am losing is the understanding that we have had between us."

"And I don't understand why you've been such a pest."

"You have given me no choice. What am I supposed to do? Be absolutely quiet while Priscilla Peanut Butter and

Berkowitz and Karen and everyone in the whole of this world accuse me of taking things that don't belong to you? I can't be quiet even if you can be. Even if you choose to sleep the whole thing off. You'd hide inside a test tube if you'd fit. Well, most of the problems in this life won't fit inside a damn test tube. And if you crawl inside one at the age of twelve, you'll cramp your growth. No wonder I'm upset. And I intend to continue being upset."

"And upset my mother and upset Marilyn and upset my father and Mr. Berkowitz and if you keep at it, you'll upset the principal at Astra and that will be a wonderful upset. That will let them toss out the whole science program. Enough of the equipment was returned to forget the whole thing. The rest of the equipment will turn up at the end of the year."

"Ben, don't tune me out. Don't tune out what I'm telling you. Listen to me. Those thefts are only a symptom. The two of us can figure this out, the way that we always work things out together. You find out about the amides for William's project. Look it up."

"We just got home, remember? I'm sorry if I don't have a handy dandy branch of the Dupont Library in the next room. I'm terribly sorry, George, if you might have to wait a few more hours before you get the information."

"I'll wait until tomorrow. They say that two heads are better than one."

"Even when one is simple minded?"

"Simple minded? You call me simple minded?"

"I meant . . ."

"*I* say that one head has to do the work of two when one of them is stuffed with cotton and chemistry. Cotton and chemistry."

"I meant to say *single* minded."

"Yeah. Cotton, to keep out the sounds of the world and chemistry to keep out its smell."

"You didn't even listen to what I said. I said that I meant single minded."

"Yeah, well, I meant what I said I said. Cotton and chemistry."

Then Ben exploded, "For crying out loud, George, you're crying out loud."

"Crying?" George screamed, before Ben interrupted with, "Oh, shut up, George! Shut up already."

And George did shut up. He shut up right then. And almost immediately *then,* Ben became sorry that he had ever asked that of George.

seven

A<small>T 9:30 BEN AND MRS. CARR</small> arrived at the office of the psychiatrist. They had been asked to come a half hour early for their first visit so that the nurse, who wore the tightest, pinkest uniform that Ben had ever seen, could fill out forms on everything that Ben told her and everything that his mother told her, too. The nurse asked if there were any siblings: one. Name and age: Howard, eight. Was delivery normal? As normal as the U.S. Mail and more punctual. To whom should the bill be sent? To Mrs. Marilyn Carr; her husband would take care of the whole thing. Ben thought that George would enjoy hearing that.

Dr. Herrold appeared to be a reasonable man. Friendly, too. Ben decided that he would tell him about George. Knowing about George would clear everything up immediately. It would save his own reputation and also save his father a lot of money. Ben realized that having George live inside of him was not normal, but it was a fact. Since Dr. Herrold was a psychiatrist, he was practically a scientist and would have to accept reality, the reality of George.

So right at first, right at the beginning of Dr. Herrold's first conversation with Ben, Ben said, "Dr. Herrold, I would like to save us this trouble. I would like to clear this whole thing up immediately. I know that doctors can keep a confidence. Howard is the only other person who knows. If you look at the record, you'll see that Howard is my sibling. I must request that you not tell anyone else."

Dr. Herrold replied, "Ben, if we're going to get anywhere at all with this relationship, it has to be based on mutual trust."

"Right," Ben said. "It will be very upsetting to others if you tell them. Especially Marilyn. Marilyn is the second wife of my father. She is also the mother of Frederica who is a patient of your college roommate's. Marilyn would be very upset to learn about George." Dr. Herrold did not interrupt; psychiatrists don't. Ben paused, waiting for Dr. Herrold to ask.

When Dr. Herrold realized that Ben was waiting, he asked, "Who is George?" He asked it gently as he scanned Ben's records.

"You won't find George on the charts. George is the little man who lives inside of me. He's really a good friend of mine. My best friend, as a matter of fact. And he is

(95)

amusing. He swears sometimes, but he says funny things, too."

Dr. Herrold gave no look of shock. Ben should have known. The doctor's look was one of patience and understanding. If Dr. Herrold had realized the importance of what Ben was saying, he would at least have looked surprised. Dr. Herrold thought that he knew about such things. They were rare, but it was his job to talk his patients out of them. After many therapy sessions. He calmly asked, "Does George talk to you at any special times, Ben?"

"No, but he talks in a special way. He can talk to me silently or out loud. When he wants to say something to Howard, he'll talk out loud. And he was being very upset about the thefts in the lab when he accidentally talked out loud at Marilyn's.

"Do you think that George would talk to me, Ben?"

Ben smiled and said, "George? George, Dr. Herrold will let me stop therapy and live with Mother if you explain to him that I am not a schizo and that you are really there."

Doctor and patient focussed on Ben's stomach. Nothing. Ben realized that if George had meant to cooperate, he would never even have had to make the request out loud in front of Dr. Herrold. "George!" he urged, looking down at his stomach, something he had never done before when he spoke to his little man. Never ever done before. "George," he repeated. "C'mon now, don't be stubborn.

Talk to Dr. Herrold."

Dr. Herrold cleared his throat. "Does George often not do as you ask him to?"

Ben heard the tolerance in the voice of the doctor, and he knew that he was tolerantly misunderstood. (I believe in you, Ben, but I don't believe you. Again. Again.)

Ben heard himself saying, "The sore sport. We've always gotten along until this year; it was always just understood between us, and now he's mad because last night I told him to shut up." And as Ben listened to himself, he heard disbelief fall—*plunk, plunk*—onto the desk that separated Dr. L. Daniel Herrold and Benjamin Dickinson Carr.

Dr. Herrold asked Ben to describe what had made him tell George to shut up, and Ben spent the rest of his first session with his psychiatrist explaining in a very orderly and logical fashion about the thefts in the school laboratory and how those had evolved into last night's argument. Then they made an appointment for a week from Saturday, the first Saturday after the New Year, and for every Saturday, 10:00 A.M., after that. Saturday was the one day that Mrs. Carr did not work, and the doctor did.

As Ben and his mother left the office, they drove past Astra. In the school parking lot Ben noticed the red Mustang that meant Cheryl and William were in the lab doing their thing.

Ben said to his mother what he usually saved to say to

George, "I wish I could do research during Christmas vacation. Those seniors are lucky."

"So are you," his mother added. "You're lucky to have someone as gifted as Mr. Berkowitz and as interested as he is to teach all of you. That makes you lucky, too. It was wonderful of him to arrange all of it."

Ben said, "I could do what the seniors are doing. I could keep up with them. If I had a car and could get to the lab whenever I wanted to, I'd be there all the time. Weekends and vacations."

"If you had a car? What good would that do you? You're not old enough to drive. Besides, if Mr. Berkowitz thought that all the kids in the class should be allowed to do research, he would have arranged it that way instead of the way he did."

"Even if he had arranged for me to do research and even if I had a car, I'll bet that I'd still never get a chance to do it. I'd be busy driving to the supermarket and picking up Howard from the Sandlers' and driving to the dry cleaners. All that I would be allowed to do if I could drive would be to do more errands for you."

"You talk as if you are being deprived of the Nobel Prize because you have to do a few things around the house."

"William and Cheryl never have to. And even Karen who is poorer than we are, at least poorer than Dad, doesn't have to."

"What do they have to do?"

"Get good grades. Get into a good college. Grow. Have fun. That is all they have to do. All they have to do when they are at home is to BE."

"What do they have to be, Ben?"

Ben waved his arm and flapped his hand. "Be themselves. That's all. That's all that is asked of them."

Charlotte Carr could not look at her son because she was driving, but she wished that she could. She spoke very softly and seriously. "Ben they are not being asked to be themselves. They are being asked to be *everything*. Everything except members of their families. They think that William and Cheryl must make contact with everything outside their homes to find what they have inside themselves." A red light. Mrs. Carr looked at her Ben and added, "I think that they're afraid of asking their children to do something unimportant because they think that will stop them from doing something important. How about Archimedes discovering the principles of buoyancy while taking a bath."

Ben was impatient with explanations, with the truth. "Taking a bath, yes, but he ran out without washing out the tub. I'll bet that if I said to you, 'Mother, I am on my way to the lab because I am on the verge of discovering the relationship between the hydrogen bomb and halitosis,' you would say, 'That's cute, Ben, but take out the garbage before you leave.'"

Mrs. Carr laughed. "I hate the word *cute*. I'd say, 'That's *nice,*' and I'd say *please* when I asked you to take out the garbage."

Ben continued, "And if I said, 'Mother, I have to leave this minute or all the equipment will disintegrate,' you would say, 'Talk about disintegration, that garbage is beginning to stink. The equipment can wait a minute, but the garbagemen won't.' "

"No," Mrs. Carr insisted, "now, that I wouldn't do. I might suggest that you take out the garbage on the way to the lab, but I would let Howie do it if you really didn't have the time; and if he weren't around, I would do it myself. I respect your work more than I do the garbage."

Ben gave his mother a cold look. She caught it and realized that he was not ready to make a joke of the situation. She was worried. Ben had always been unsettled after a visit to Marilyn's. In the past, she had waited for his blues to go, but now she wondered how she should handle her son. Maybe the psychiatrist would tell her that she wasn't allowed to argue with a child in therapy. She wanted to be reassuring, "Doesn't it make you proud to realize how important you are to our family. That is, to our family here in Lawton Beach?"

"Important?" Ben grunted. "That doesn't make me important. One uneducated, full-time Mr. Clean could unimportant me right out of the house." He paused, then added, "I'll tell you what it does, though. It sure makes me peculiar at school. I'm the only kid at Astra who wheels groceries home in a cart and who knows the price of dry cleaning a lady's skirt. Now, you take William. He *is* important to his mother. She happens to think that he is something great, and she never puts garbage or dirty dishes in the way of his being great."

"It never seemed to bother you before this year," Charlotte Carr said.

They pulled into the carport. Mrs. Carr shut off the motor. Ben added, "It never did bother me before this year. I never thought much about what other kids might think of me before this year. I was so busy listening to George. I was happy listening to him. And you, you happen to be lucky that George has always been on your side."

"George? George who?"

"George Carr. That George who. George, the little man who lives inside of me. I told Dr. Herrold about him this morning, but George wouldn't talk to him. And he probably won't talk to you, either, even though he's always been on your side and has always made me take out the garbage and keep everyone in the family on time."

"Did George ever tell you to do something that you didn't want to do?"

"Mother, it is just that kind of thinking that has me in the trouble that I'm in now. Right now."

"Sorry, Ben. Take it easy. I don't understand what kind of thinking you are talking about."

"Thinking that George is responsible for all the thefts in the lab." And with that, Ben marched into the house and sat at his desk for a long time listening. Thinking and listening. Until his mother called him and asked him to go with Howard to the Qwik-Chek for a loaf of bread for supper.

Mrs. Carr waited until Ben and Howard had gone to buy the loaf of bread that she didn't need before she called Dr. Herrold. After thinking back and further back, she had remembered that George had been the name of Ben's imaginary friend in the time before he had started school. In the long ago before Howard was born. Before their father left home. Was her son so emotionally disturbed that he had re-invented George, an imaginary creature from a happier time, from a time when his father was around the house? She told Dr. Herrold over the phone all she knew of George, and she told him how worried she was. He asked her to come to his office to see him. Without Ben.

eight

SCHOOL RESUMED with the usual post-holiday inertia, the tendency of a student body at rest wanting to stay at rest. Boys together and boys and girls together talked about what they had done during vacation. The girls came to school, not on the first day following vacation but on the second, wearing that which was new and which they had received from Christmas.

Ron and Lacey had made considerable progress in their research during vacation. Adam and Violet had had a little trouble, but they appeared to have enjoyed it.

William complained, "The closest that I came to a lab was the smell of alcohol in the drugstore I worked in."

"Working during vacations is also profitable," Mr. Berkowitz said.

"Only mildly so. A buck and a quarter an hour," William joked.

"Did your mother cut your allowance, William old boy?" Lacey asked.

"Nothing like that; working was my idea. Actually, I had to talk them into it."

"I think," said Mr. Berkowitz, "that having some responsibility outside of school would be helpful to a lot of people. As long as Cheryl didn't mind being held back."

"Oh, Mr. Berkowitz," Cheryl said, "I don't feel that I was held back by William. We'll make it up weekends and over the Easter holidays."

"Should I bother looking at this?" Mr. Berkowitz asked Cheryl, picking up her lab book.

Cheryl stroked her hair out of her eyes and slowly nodded no. Mr. Berkowitz handed her back her notebook without opening it. "Ah, too bad that for the two of you, the frontiers of science remained somewhere north of Lawton Beach over this vacation. In research you have to be prepared for everything, including long periods when there is no progress at all."

Cheryl brushed her hair out of her eyes and said, "You know, that is very true, Mr. Berkowitz."

And Mr. Berkowitz added, "Not only is it very true, but it also makes a good song title. *Sometimes nothing happening means that something is happening. Cha cha cha.*"

Ben thought: You have to like that guy, Berkowitz, cha cha cha. Even George liked Berkowitz. Ben knew, even though George had never discussed his feelings with him. Actually, William was the only person that they had ever disagreed about. Actually, Ben never bothered with very many kids. Actually, that may be the reason that there had been little disagreement between George and him. Well, if George couldn't take any competition at all, that showed what an incompetent he was.

He would show George. He would do the homework that George had asked him to do. He had more time lately, anyway; he wasn't busy with George and he had no other friend taking his place yet. He would learn all the details of making amides from indole compounds. (If George cared to listen and learn, he could.) And then, and then, Ben decided, he would take all that information and with it he would help William. And Cheryl. Smiling kindly, talking patiently, he would help William. And Cheryl. William would be thankful and tell Ben that he was. And Cheryl would say thank you and ask Ben if she could take Howard for a ride in the red Mustang, and Ben would let her. And that would show George. George needs me more than I need him, Ben thought. I can stay silent as long as he can. Longer. Because once I help William, he will be my friend outside of school until he goes to college. That will make George begin to talk again to make William look bad. George loves being sarcastic about William.

Ben reviewed all these thoughts later as he boarded the school bus. Cheryl drove out of the parking lot just as the bus was pulling up. William was sitting so close to her that she looked as if she had two heads. Two heads are better than one, he thought, reminding himself of the last argument he had had with George. What would George say if he told him about Cheryl's driving with William sitting so close? Ben was sure that it would be sarcastic. George would probably say something about their not making progress in the lab over Christmas because they couldn't unfasten themselves from each other to get out of the car. Then Ben would say they must have gotten unfastened because the car was empty when he saw it in the parking lot over Christmas. And then George would say how come William said that he didn't get near the lab. And then Ben would say that maybe Cheryl worked alone. And then George would say that anyway you looked at it, something was rotten because either Cheryl broke the rules and worked without a partner or else William lied and *was* in the lab. And then Ben would tell George to shut up. And then Ben stopped his thinking. Why did he lately always end with wanting to tell George to shut up?

Mrs. Carr did not mind getting off work to keep her appointment with Dr. Herrold. He couldn't fit her in until after Ben had had his second visit. *Did not mind* would hardly describe Mrs. Carr's condition. Between the time Ben had told her about George and the time she could see his doctor, she felt like a raw, pared potato, exposed and darkening. She was anxious to do the right thing, but she did not know what that might be. Mrs. Carr was as curious about George as any mother would be who suddenly discovers that either she had a third child or that her first one really has a severe problem. She never mentioned George to Ben, not because she didn't want to but because she didn't know if she ought to.

Dr. Herrold began their conversation by saying that he was not ready to make a conclusive diagnosis yet, but after only two sessions he was willing to say that Ben was not a schizophrenic.

Mrs. Carr smiled, "I hope that you will write that to Mr. Carr and address the letter to Marilyn, his present wife, living in Norfolk, Virginia."

Dr. Herrold cautioned, "Ben does have a problem even though he is not a schizophrenic. A schizophrenic is a split personality, and the split off part is out of touch with reality, with what is going on. Ben is in touch with reality. Even the George part, who can't see it, is in touch with reality."

"My son, the invisible," said Mrs. Carr.

Dr. Herrold warned Mrs. Carr not to be too optimistic. He called it optimistic, but he really meant for her not to be flip. What Ben was, he pointed out, was a multiple personality. He was two people: Person A and Person B. Dr. Jekyll and Mr. Hyde was an example. Ben was Ben, but he was also George. Sometimes people who are two people don't let one half know what the other half does. Like Dr. Jekyll didn't know about Mr. Hyde. But in Ben's case that wasn't so. And sometimes, one of the personalities does evil and the other does good. But that was not Ben's case either. Mrs. Carr sighed with relief—thinking again of the thefts in the lab. Ben knew about George, and George knew about Ben. "George has become Ben's mouthpiece. George swears while Ben smiles. With a youngster as intelligent as Ben, I think that we can clear this up in time. I am encouraged already by the fact that George has stopped speaking to Ben."

Dr. Herrold wanted to know from Mrs. Carr, Ben's reaction right after she and her husband had separated. He asked other questions—about Howard and history, personal Carr history. Mrs. Carr left the office after learning that she should talk about George only if Ben did and that she herself should take out the garbage if Ben seemed particularly annoyed at the job. Piecing together all that she had learned in Dr. Herrold's office, she realized that her son Ben was not the neat package of good adjustment that she had thought he was. He was two packages, one part invented. Howard, whom any man on the street or any teacher or any baby sitter could spot as a bundle of chaos, got everything out of his system through a well-developed opening, his mouth, his loud-o-mouth. But not Benjamin. Ben kept it all in and invented George. When Ben was disturbed, when Ben was angry, when Ben was resentful, George spoke up for him. Privately, silently George had spoken. Until he went loud and public at Marilyn's.

nine

FROM THE TIME that Ben first saw Dr. Herrold until
Easter was a time of great progress in the therapy. Dr.
Herrold had asked to see Howard.

Ben explained to his brother, "He wants to see you
because you are my sibling."

"I know what a sibling is. Raymond's mother uses
that word all the time. I don't like it much; it sounds
like it belongs to rabbits. Mrs. Sandler puts up with
me because Raymond has no sibling of his own. She
calls me a substitute sibling. Doesn't that sound like
rabbits?"

"Dr. Herrold is going to ask you about George. You
can tell him."

"You mean you told him about George? I'll bet that
George is furious. I'll bet that's why he hasn't been talking lately."

"That's only the second reason. The first reason is because I *told* him to shut up."

"Why did you do something dumb like that?"

"Private reasons."

"Shall I tell Dr. Herrold that George isn't talking to us any more?"

"Yeah. Tell him that, Howard. He'd like to hear that. That's what he has been working for."

And so Howard did. He told; he told how George had talked to him and how George had stopped. He explained; he explained when—the first time after he had been expelled from kindergarten and the other times when they were walking home from the Sandler's or discussing their chores for supper. Howard confessed; he confessed the names that George had invented for Mrs. Carr.

Dr. Herrold smiled; he smiled at it all. And he called another conference with Mrs. Carr. He again explained to her that George was Ben's way to say things that he didn't have the courage to say. He also believed that George was Ben's way of consoling himself for not having friends. Ben believed that George had not wanted him to have friends. George had not spoken to Ben or Ben to George for three and a half months. That was progress. Ben was integrating his two personalities into one strong one. Dr. Herrold believed that they could safely cut down on the number of visits, and he had mentioned that in his last letter to Mr. Carr. He further explained that Mr. Carr was quite anxious to see the progress that Ben has made.

"I have no objection to his visiting his dad. It is wonderful to work with such an intelligent boy and with such cooperative parents," he concluded.

"What about Howard?" Mrs. Carr asked.

"Oh, yes, Howard. He certainly speaks up. He is a little loud, but I think that he will learn to control that in time."

"What I meant was, what about Howard visiting his father with Ben?"

"Oh, yes. By all means, Mrs. Carr. Howard will add to the normalcy of the situation for Ben. We want to test, but we are not ready to stress. Do you understand what I mean by that, Mrs. Carr?"

Mrs. Carr nodded yes, she understood, so Dr. Herrold explained anyway. "We want to test, but not to stress," he resumed. "Too much stress, too much pressure, too much responsibility may bring about George's return. We don't want that. And I believe that I may safely say that now Ben doesn't want that either."

And so in view of George's longtime silence, plans were made for Ben and Howard to visit Dad and Marilyn and their half-sibling, Frederica, just as they always did at Easter time. All in view of Ben's progress. On the Saturday before Easter recess would begin, Dr. Herrold probed and prodded Ben; he asked if he missed George. Ben lied and said no. Dr. Herrold pronounced him ready for Marilyn, and he smiled as Ben left the office.

Ben did not smile. He felt nasty; what grown-ups call irritable. He wanted a fight with someone; what grown-ups call hostile. He felt picked on and put upon; what grown-ups call frustrated.

As they passed Astra, Ben put all those feelings into focus, turned to his mother and said, "I'd like you to stop the car so that I can stop in the lab for a minute." He looked straight out the windshield before he added, "Please."

Mrs. Carr decided that all the dark notes in his voice and manner would grow if she answered in the same tone, so she said lightly, as lightly as she could, "I hope you won't be too long; I've got to do the laundry today."

Ben sat with his arms folded across his chest, not moving. "If it's too much trouble for you to stop for me, forget it."

"It's really no trouble to stop. As a matter of fact, we *are* stopped. I'd hate to have to wait too long, though. I need to catch up on the laundry today so that you will have clean clothes to take to Norfolk."

"If you're going to rush me, I won't bother at all."

"Go on in, Ben. How will fifteen minutes be?"

"I don't know how they'll be. They may not be enough." Ben did not move from the car.

"Well, try fifteen," Mrs. Carr said. "If they aren't enough, come back out and tell me. I'll go home, do the laundry and come back for you."

Ben got out of the car and poked his head in through the open window. "I'll try to finish in *twenty* minutes. But you wait. Don't leave without telling me."

Ben walked toward the school entrance he always took, hoping that he would find it locked. Then he wouldn't have to prepare an opening remark for when he walked into the lab. The clever things that he thought to himself after he was in bed needed to be modified for an audience, especially an audience as special as William, who was about to become his friend.

Ben had thought about William's project. And Cheryl's. He had studied and sorted out their troubles, what they had claimed were their troubles and which they had described to Mr. Berkowitz. Ben had questioned Mr. B. about them when he was over at his house one Saturday night. Mr. Berkowitz was usually at their home on Saturday nights. Besides, he often stopped in for coffee during the week. Mrs. Carr had taken to clearing the dishes from the table right after supper, but she still did the crossword puzzle before she washed them.

If George had given Ben any indication at all that he was ready to make up, Ben would have happily discussed William's project with him. But he didn't, so Ben had had to think it out alone. Ben was pleased that he had successfully thought through a problem without George's help. Of course, the problem had merely been one of sorting information and putting it in good order. George had been better at solving problems that involved a crazy way of looking at things. George was crazy. Not him. Not Benjamin Dickinson Carr.

Ben could have discussed his idea with Mr. Berkowitz

several times. Any of the times that he had come over for coffee or the time he had brought records from his apartment. He had brought them to share and not because he didn't have a record player of his own. But Ben didn't want to talk it over with Mr. Berkowitz. That would be a lesser form of charity: to help and let everyone know that you had helped. Besides, since Ben had lost contact with George, what William thought mattered more to him than what Mr. Berkowitz or his mother or any other adult in the world thought.

And now, his mother had stopped the car; Ben was at the front door of the school, and it was not locked. He would have to tell William and Cheryl. It would help if he could think of a very clever opening sentence. He didn't have to.

As he approached the lab, he heard Cheryl singing. Singing, moaning, and giggling all together and all apart. The moans were from the throat, and the giggle from her head. Her eyes looked like the punched-out holes in two-ring notebook paper. Dark and strangely unblinking. She looked as if she were cooking on the inside with something that was pulling all the moisture from her skin. Bright but powdery.

"What's the matter with you, Cheryl?" became Ben's opening remark.

"Which *me* are you referring to? To the one who is here or to the one who is tiptoeing around the ceiling?"

Ben answered with a puzzled look to William. Were

they making fun of him? Did they know about George? William put his arm around Ben's shoulder. "She's upset because we have failed again. I was just taking down our equipment. She'll be all right."

Ben continued staring at Cheryl who was now picking lint, invisible lint, or bugs, invisible bugs from her slacks. William interrupted Ben's line of sight by standing in front of him as he asked, "Is there some special reason why you came to school today?"

Ben tried peeking around William at Cheryl. She was a sight, with her head weaving as if her neck had been injected with Jello.

"Is there something special you wanted, Ben?"

"Well, I have a plan for your project. Your research, William."

"Oh, we're going to give up. It won't affect our grades anyway. We're quitting. Nothing else doing for the rest of vacation. I was taking everything down now to clean it up and return it all to Mr. Berkowitz when we get back to school."

William suddenly turned around and dashed over to where Cheryl was gazing at the glowing coils of a small electric heater. She stretched her arm to touch it, and William pulled it away from her by the cord. Cheryl acted as if he were playing, and she giggled and began to chase the heater, climbing up on the lab table and padding around on all fours to do it. William found an asbestos glove and lifted the heater off the table and brought it

to the table near where Ben stood. He noticed Ben staring at the electric heater. It was just like the one that had
been taken from the lab. It could have been it, and it
could not have been. One electric heater is the twin of
every other electric heater, except for the number taped
to the bottom.

"We were assigned this one. For our research," William
volunteered after he noticed Ben's staring.

"Why would you need that?"

"For refluxing, silly. You know that. Any long period
of reflux requires an even heat. You can't be safe with a
Bunsen burner. You should know that."

"But, William, why do you need a long reflux period?
That's what is breaking down your amide. That's why
you're not making any progress. Look, give me a piece of
paper, I'll outline my idea."

William acted interested and began searching the contents of his drawers for a piece of paper, something that
wasn't bound into his lab notebook. As he opened one
drawer and then another, Cheryl sang, sitting on the lab
table, two tables away. She sounded as if she were eight-
een tables away and in the next room. Ben noticed a beautiful array of equipment as one drawer and then the next
was flashed open. A fractionating column, even more
dear than a condenser, a separating funnel. Yes, that
would be necessary to separate the water solution from
the ethyl alcohol. . . . But no, ethyl alcohol and water
mix completely; they would have to be separated by distil-

(*117*)

lation. They didn't need a separating funnel. Ben noticed an opened box of sugar cubes; and William, seeing that Ben noticed, told Ben that they made coffee in the lab, and that, actually, if Ben really wanted to know, that was why they had the electric heater in the first place. William said that he knew that a long reflux period would break down the amide. William said that now their secret was out. He told Ben that he would appreciate it if he never said anything to anyone about their making coffee. He winked. The Board of Education might not understand their using materials to heat water for Instant Maxwell House. All that electricity down the drain, ha, ha, he added.

"Where's the coffee?" Ben asked, glancing in the cupboard.

"We're fresh out. Used the last of it this morning." Strange that all the coffee should be gone but only one sugar cube missing. Ben looked in the wastebasket, wondering where the empty jar was. Ben answered himself, explaining that they would not want to leave an empty jar around for the janitor to discover. Probably Cheryl had put it in her purse, that huge pouch she wore over her shoulder. William asked, "Now, what was I looking for?"

"A piece of paper."

"Oh, yes," William said.

Ben noticed a bottle of methyl alcohol. "This alcohol may be your problem, William," Ben volunteered.

"Oh, yes," William laughed. "You mean Cheryl?"

"I hope that I don't mean Cheryl. She didn't drink any of this, did she? This is wood alcohol. You know that. It makes people go blind."

William blushed, "I thought you meant the way that Cheryl was acting."

"No, I meant *your* reaction. Your research. You should use ethyl alcohol."

"Oh, yes. Yes. I do. We do. We do that, Ben. We use the other. The one you said. We use ethyl. The safe kind to drink."

"Then why do you have the methyl?"

"Oh, just some odds and ends that I picked up while I was working at the drugstore over Christmas. We seem to use alcohol up so fast." William looked over at Cheryl again.

"Picked up?" Ben repeated. He didn't like the idea that was coming into his head about the relationship between their using up so much alcohol and Cheryl's singsong manner.

"Well, bought. You know, the school is so funny about letting you have alcohol. You have to account for every drop of it. So I bought this. Wholesale. Like part of my pay. Stupid me, though, I bought the wrong stuff. I thought I could substitute. Dumb, wasn't it?"

"It must have been pretty cheap if you didn't even try to take it back."

"Well, I said that it was wholesale. A fringe benefit, you might say. Like getting paid a dollar and a quarter an hour plus tips for delivering isn't all that much."

"Did you buy this other stuff there, too? This ergot stuff?"

William laughed, "Yes, I was so sure that I'd be blazing trails for science that I went ahead and bought that; it has an indole base, and I wanted to make an amide of it."

"You must have been successful. The ergot container is almost empty," Ben said, shaking it.

"Oh, we tried, but it spilled. Yeah. Knocked it over. Pretty near the whole thing spilled out. Luckily, it was soluble in water. Washed the whole thing right down the sink. Just like the lady said, right down the drain." William slammed the drawer shut. "How about jotting your idea down on a paper towel. No, you don't want to do that. Benjamin, I can't seem to find a single scrap of paper. Why don't you do this? Why don't you write all those products of your teeming little brain, ha ha, teeming *big* brain down on a letter and send them to me? I'll be home over Easter. You'll be at your dad's, won't you? The mail will go through. Good old U.S. Mail. You send me your ideas. Yeah, Ben, I think that is the best idea I've had today. It just may be the best research idea ever."

He turned Ben around by the shoulders and led him out of the lab, away from Cheryl who was lying on the lab table and staring at the ceiling and smiling at it very hard. Ben turned around only briefly and said, "I hate to interfere or anything, William, but I hope that you aren't going to let Cheryl drive home."

"I'll handle that. Don't worry about it, Ben. Just don't tell. That silly girl just got too upset about things. Don't you think you can take things too seriously?"

"Well, I take school seriously. And research. And using certain chemicals the way that they are supposed to be used. Like no wonder they make you sign out for alcohol. Like I don't think that you should get methyl alcohol from a drugstore so that you can maybe drink the ethyl alcohol."

"Ben," William said in a very solemn manner, "please take my word for it. Alcohol has nothing, I repeat, nothing, to do with what is bothering Cheryl right now. I promise to drive her home immediately, if you'll promise not to tell anyone about how she is acting. Not anyone, like the man who happens to be teaching this course and who happens to be romancing your mother."

"What has Mr. Berkowitz's visiting my mother have to do with anything?"

"It should have nothing to do with anything, Ben. And I hope that it does have nothing to do with anything. Because it would be unfair to take advantage of your position to whisper things that you aren't even sure about to Mr. Berkowitz."

"I've got to go," Ben said. "And I think you ought to leave right now, too. My mother has to do the laundry."

"I'm going." William began to guide Cheryl toward the door. "Yeah, Ben, you go, too, and help your mother with the laundry."

"The laundry," Ben said, "she does all by herself. Except for the sheets, which she sends out." Ben realized that what he was saying was foolish, but it was out like a vapor, shapeless and uncontained.

"Well, that is just wonderful, Ben. Your li'l ole mother is just a real great li'l ole gal." William said as he guided Cheryl through the lab door. "No wonder Berkowitz likes her so much." The last he said as a reminder to Ben, and Ben knew it. Ben turned and walked rapidly down the corridor; he heard Cheryl singing and following behind. He rushed out of the school and into the car before Cheryl and William had finished weaving their way down the hall.

Mrs. Carr was disappointed that Ben did not leave his bad mood in the laboratory. It was still with him when he returned to the car, but it had shifted its focus from her to something else. Something he wasn't telling her about.

Ben wanted George to talk to him. Here was a problem. Here was something that needed analysis. Here was a situation that was more than its parts. George and William naturally repelled each other, and Ben who was an unattached opposite charge did not know whether he wanted to pair with one or the other. As he had pulled toward William, George had turned him loose. Now that William had been repulsive, Ben wanted George. Ben had always wanted George.

But not a chirp or whistle, not a sound from there.

ten

M<small>R. BERKOWITZ EMERGED</small> from his Volkswagen in parts. Legs first and then the drape of his stomach. Then his moustache, his arm, and the bottle of wine attached to that. It was seven o'clock but still light enough for Howard and Raymond to be playing in the carport.

Howard asked, "Why do you think that a big guy like him drives such a small car? He looks like a dumb eggplant."

"That's probably the only kind of car that he can afford," Ray said.

"I'll bet he flaps over onto the other seat on one side and chafes his leg against the door on the other. I'll bet he has to kneesies his dumb self to be able to shift gears. I'm going to get a car with a floor shift. As soon as I have my moustache."

"What are you having for supper tonight?" Ray asked.

"Him," Howard said staring as Mr. Berkowitz walked up the path from the curb to their home.

"I mean what are you going to eat?"

"We bought chicken, and we'll have rice and salad. And the salad won't be from a plastic bag either. We bought a whole ball of lettuce and stuff."

"My mother does that all the time. She breaks up lettuce and shreds cabbage," Ray said. "My mother even fixes peas that come in pods not in cans or cartons. My mother bakes cakes, and she once baked bread even. My mother makes her own spaghetti sauce and . . ."

Howard said, "Go home, Raymond."

Raymond left.

When Howard walked inside, he noticed that his mother had set the table with a table cloth instead of place mats and had taken the bread out of its wrapper and put it on a plate.

"Well, la-de-dah, fancy," he said.

Mrs. Carr wished for the thirty-first time that day that she could develop a severe case of packed wax in her ears. She smiled an arc of a smile that showed no teeth and patted her son on the top of his head. She tapped Howard on his shoulder, and smiling still, moved her clenched fist under his jaw, "Mr. Berkowitz is going to fix the salad tonight, boys. It's one of his specialties. Caesar salad."

Howard's eyes went toward the ceiling, "If it's anything like that goop that Marilyn makes with raisins and carrots, tell him to forget it."

Mrs. Carr's hand cupped Howard's mouth as she pressed him to her. A muzzle, a muzzle. A jaw strap. Teeth braces locked together. "Caesar salad is what we had that night Mr. Berkowitz took us to the restaurant." Howard removed his mother's hand from his mouth.

"And that's the one that makes Marilyn's the second worst in the whole world. Because that one was the first worst. The dumb waiter broke a raw egg into it. Remember? Yicch. He brought all the dumb stuff over on a cart, and the egg was in a dish and when he broke it, it wasn't even cooked."

Mrs. Carr said, "Sit down, Howard."

The meal was a success, and Mr. Berkowitz was an appreciative eater. Howard skipped the salad. After dessert Mrs. Carr mentioned that she was planning on flying to New Jersey over Easter recess. She would leave a number for the boys to call if they needed her.

"Why New Jersey?" Ben asked.

"Yeah, what's there?" Howard added.

"Well, for one thing," Mrs. Carr began slowly, "that huge crowd of college kids is *not* there. Why, they've already started coming in—crowding the roads and cluttering the beaches. Now, that's something to think about." She looked at Howard and Ben and saw that they needed another reason. After all, they were her sons. She wouldn't have believed such nonsense either. So she cleared her throat and added, "And I would like to meet Mrs. Berkowitz."

"You know there ain't no Mrs. Berkowitz; he," Howard said pointing to Mr. Berkowitz, "ain't even married."

"No," his mother agreed, "but his mother was, and her name happens to be Mrs. Berkowitz."

"Why would you want to visit some old lady?" Howard asked. He stretched his upper and lower lips so that they folded over his teeth and hid them. Pumping his gums up and down and making all his *s*'s as wet as spit and bad manners could make them, he said, "Well, s-s-sonnie, how's-s-s it going down there in the S-s-sunshine S-s-state?"

Charlotte Carr got up from the table, grabbed the back of Howard's chair, and tipped it forward until its eight year old contents spilled. Then she rubbed her hands together and said, "Well, Sheldon, for better or for worse."

And Howard, who could always guess what was coming on television and who could always tell when the villain had gone one step too far, Howard who always knew his limits said, "Sheldon! Sheldon! That's your name? Your actual name? What a dumb sissy name. D-U-M sissy name." And Howard sat on the floor where he had been spilled, and with his hands supporting him and his legs splayed in a wide V, he turned his head around and asked his mother in words that came like bruises, "Are you going to marry him, Ma? Are you?"

Mrs. Carr's eyes filled with tears; she realized that Howard had known his limits, but he couldn't stay within them. Howard was upset, loud and upset, and Charlotte

Carr knew that she had upset him long before she had tipped his chair over. She said, "Sheldon and I have thought about it, Howie; we were going to decide over this vacation. There are a lot of things to consider." She looked at Ben, her dear Ben, whose quiet ways had made him a second thought.

Ben was waiting to be noticed. By Mother. By George. But George remained silent, and so did Ben.

His mother asked, "What are you thinking, Ben?"

Such openings Ben usually reserved for George alone, so he substituted, "I was thinking that dumb is spelled D-U-M-B, and that not knowing how to spell it, makes you it." He looked at Howard.

Sheldon Berkowitz said, "Dumb also means silent, and it's spelled the same way."

"Anyway you spell it, that meaning will never apply to Howard McHune Carr," Charlotte smiled.

"Is McHune your middle name, Howie?" Mr. Berkowitz asked.

"Yeah, it's a old family name on my father's side. I hate it. As soon as I get old enough to have a moustache, I'm going to change it to Ferrari."

"Ferrari, like the sports car?"

"Yeah. Howard Ferrari Carr. That's got class."

"And that may be the only way you'll ever own a Ferrari car," said Mr. Berkowitz, laughing.

They all laughed. Ben, too. Even though no one noticed at first.

Ben lay awake. His mother and Mr. Berkowitz probably had their minds made up already. They would get married. It would be all right having Mr. Berkowitz around all of the time. Maybe he would eventually come to treat Ben the same way that he treated Howard. Ben didn't know if Mr. Berkowitz acted cautious with him because he was shy outside the classroom or because he knew about Dr. Herrold. Ben wished he didn't have to visit his father. He had never liked pineapple glazed ham for Easter, and at Marilyn's you not only got it but you had to make a fuss over how pretty it looked. Marilyn's parents would be there, fussing over Frederica and treating him as if he were recovering from jungle rot. Everyone except Freddie would be interested in his progress, wanting to know but not wanting to ask. He would make them ask. He wouldn't volunteer one piece of information.

And he wouldn't write to William, either. George didn't have to tell him that William and Cheryl weren't working on research in the lab. They didn't care any more about scientific progress than Frederica cared about psychological progress. William must have cared earlier in the year, though. Going to the trouble to get all that stuff from the drugstore. Methyl alcohol. Ergot.

Knock. Knock.

Who's there?

Ergot.

Ergot who?

Ergot sixpence, jolly, jolly sixpence.

He waited to hear if George would moan at that pun. George didn't.

If he didn't have to worry about people thinking that he was crazy, he'd get up right then and look up *ergot*. He couldn't remember the formula.

Good grief! He didn't have to worry. No one could see him. He could get up and look it up in his chemistry book.

And so Ben did.

But he didn't find it.

Ergot is not a chemical to be studied in any elementary organic chemistry course. Ben went to the encyclopedia, and there in Volume 8: Edward to Extract, he found what he needed to know. He did not have to read beyond the very beginning to know what he had to do. He ran to his brother's room and woke him.

"That was the shortest night I've ever had," Howard complained.

"It's not over. C'mon get up. I need your help."

"If the night ain't finished, my help will have to wait until it is."

"It can't. Come. Get dressed. Don't wake Mother."

"I'm up," Howard said as he turned over.

Ben shook him. "You're still horizontal." Ben began flicking the light on and off. On and off.

"How can I find my way out of bed with those lights blinking on and off like a dumb railroad crossing." Howard did get up; Ben handed his brother his pants.

"Just put your clothes on over your pajamas. I'll tell

you what it's all about in the car."

"I can't fit my pants over my pajamas," Howard said as he did exactly that. He paused as he was pulling them up. He frowned to himself and zipped. He slipped on his shoes and frowned again. He tied one shoe, frowned, tied the other and scratched his head. Then he said, "You said that you'll tell me in the car?"

"Yeah. C'mon now," Ben urged.

"And you also said, 'Don't wake Mother'?"

"Yeah. C'mon now."

"Ben, do you mind telling me who is going to drive the car? Like do you mind telling me?"

"Shshshsh. We are. C'mon now. We've got to hurry."

"We are? You are and me are?"

"Yeah. C'mon now. I need your help. I'll work the pedals, and you'll sit on my lap and steer. I can't do everything. You know more about cars than I do."

"Where are we going?"

"To Astra," Ben answered.

"Do you mind, I mean do you mind telling me why we are going to Astra?"

"I'll tell you in the car. C'mon already, How."

How c'moned.

They quietly left the house taking with them the keys that were in the bowl on the dining room table and leaving open Volume 8 of the Encyclopedia Britannica where in the right hand column was the entry that had sent them into the night.

ERGOT, a fungal disease of grasses, especially rye, that induces the transformation of the grain into enlarged, hard, beanlike structures that constitute the drug ergot, used in obstetrics. Poisoning may occur from eating ergot in flour. Ergot is the source of the powerful synthetic hallucinogen *d*-lysergic acid diethylamide, or LSD–25.

The cubes of sugar, the electric heater were not being used to make coffee at all. The electric heater would be used to reflux the ergot, and the sugar cubes would be pellets to contain the product. William and Cheryl didn't use the methy alcohol to substitute for ethyl because they were drinking the ethyl alcohol as Ben had at first suspected. Of course William could say that alcohol had nothing to do with Cheryl's problem. Nothing *directly* to do with it. Methyl alcohol was used to manufacture LSD. Merely that! And Cheryl had merely, merrily sampled their product. Ben got the shudders when he thought of it.

Once Howard was in the car, he was in command, and he stopped nagging altogether. Getting the car started and going took all of his concentration. Ben sat behind the wheel, and Howard sat on Ben. Ben didn't know what to do, and Howard who did, couldn't reach.

"I'll turn the key, and you press the gas. The gas pedal, Ben." They tried once and then twice and then Howard lost patience. "You do when I do, Ben."

He turned around as far as he could and breathed into his brother's face. He squirmed back so that he could face the windshield; he wiggled so that he could find someplace to dangle his legs comfortably. He squirmed again, and a voice came from within his brother, Ben, "Why don't you keep your face to the front and ride your bottom a bit higher and then maybe . . ."

"George!" Ben yelled. "You're back. You're back, George. Gosh, I've missed you."

"What do you mean *back?*"

"You mean you knew all along about William and didn't want to tell me?"

George answered, "If you had been any slower, I would have had to speak up. You know that you're not going to be a minute too soon. They're counting on getting the stuff from the lab and selling it to the college crowd. Probably charge five dollars per sugar cube."

"They sure don't need the money. Why do you think they're doing it, George?"

"They don't want to sell LSD as much as they want to buy their way into the next thing there is—the college crowd. They have no identity, Ben, so they work hard at being different from their group. They don't realize that they're just trying to fit into another group. The crowd may be different, but they're not."

Howard interrupted, "Ben, if you want to get this car going, you've got to cooperate." Howard turned the key in the ignition again. Ben pressed the gas pedal and

clutch, Howard shifted into reverse, and everything worked. There passed out of the Carr driveway, the strangest sight that has ever been seen since the musicians of Bremen scared away the robbers; for there sat Ben on the seat of the car, pushing pedals to the commands of Howard who was sitting on his lap, and between requests to brake it and whoa it, there was one voice saying "got ya" and a deeper one complaining, "You know he stole that stuff. That ergot and that methyl alcohol."

"Now, George, give William the benefit of the doubt."

"Ben, there can be no doubt. Can you imagine any drugstore owner selling that stuff to a kid?"

"I've got to drive now, George," Ben said.

Howard said, "Yeah, George. You can leave the driving to us."

The car with its tiered driver took all the back roads on the way to Astra. They avoided traffic, cops, and any possible chance that they might have had to put the car into reverse. Thankfully, the school parking lot was empty. Ben hoped that William had had no chance to remove everything from the lab. He hoped that William had been too busy getting Cheryl home. That very evening the college crowd was beginning to assemble on the beaches. He hoped that William had delayed opening for business.

Ben and Howard walked across the parched lawn. The grass in Florida is thick bladed and surprisingly noisy when it is dry. Like tufted paper.

Ben said, "Shshsh."

George whispered, "Do you want this operation done delicately, or do you want it done?"

Ben answered, "Both."

There was no reason for them to try entering through the door that Ben always went through. No reason except habit and hope. But the school was locked. They had to break a pane of a window to unlock it before entering. The windows were low to the ground and climbing in was easy, too. Ben knew the lab so well that he led Howard directly to the lockers that needed emptying, and that they did. Quickly. Quietly. Completely. There was no time to sort and assemble. The unused portions would be returned in their original containers as soon as possible. It took them only two trips each.

"I must say that you're using your head more lately, Ben."

"Thanks, George. I have to warn you, though; if we get caught, I'm blaming it all on you."

"That's what I call a real welcome back. Thanks a lot, Ben."

"Well, let's hope that it doesn't happen."

But it did.

It happened as they were driving back home.

The cop who first saw the Carr's car was Patrolman Hooper. He never minded having his leave canceled and going on overtime during Easter vacation. Canceling leaves and putting up One Way signs to control the invading armada was part of the Easter tradition in Lawton Beach. In Lawton Beach where a new Easter bonnet usually meant a new swimcap and where the Easter parade took place on the beach instead of on a boulevard and where Easter Bunnies wore bikinis.

Patrolman Hooper was in good spirits as he tacked up One Way signs along San Juan Avenue and the other roads that were parallel to Highway A1A and the ocean. He had just finished putting up one of them and was standing back to see whether the one end flapped too much to withstand the breezes of the sea as well as the sea of autos of the next few days. Highway A1A would be northbound and San Juan Avenue would be southbound for five miles for the next five days. He flagged the driver down by standing in the middle of the road, smiling and waving. The rules had just this minute been changed. He wanted to give the driver a reminder. Nothing more. The car continued its approach. Slowly to be sure, but approaching still. Patrolman Hooper hopped to the side of the road and blew his whistle. Cars usually stopped immediately, but how could Patrolman Hooper know that Howard could see and that Ben could not? The sounds of Patrolman Hooper's whistle drowned out the sounds of *Brake it and clutch it. Whoa, Ben. Brake and clutch. Brake and clutch. There's a cop, Ben. A cop.*

Patrolman Hooper had stopped smiling by the time the car stopped. Patrolman Hooper frowned as he approached the car. Patrolman Hooper opened his mouth in disbelief when he looked inside the car and saw two drivers—one on top of the other—and he heard three voices. Ben, Howard and George all had something to say. George had a lot to say; he knew that he would be blamed.

Patrolman Hooper simply said, "I don't believe it." And then he repeated what he had just very simply said. "I don't believe it." He nodded no and nodded no again and muttered, "This is only number one. This is only the beginning."

Ben said to Howard, "Don't you think you ought to shut out the lights and turn off the ignition?"

Howard answered, "I am. I dumb well am."

George said, "Hurry up, for crying out loud. Hurry so that you can get off of Ben's lap."

Patrolman Hooper said, "All right, you guys. Let me see your driver's license. Licenses. Both of them."

"You lose," Howard explained. "We don't have one."

Patrolman Hooper hated wise guys. "O.K., you guys. Get outta there, you guys. Give me your names and address." He wet the tip of his ballpoint pen with his tongue before he wrote. It left a comma of blue on his lower lip. He shook his head from time to time and finally said, "You mean you guys have the nerve to drive piggyback and not have a license between you."

George answered, "Officer, you wouldn't believe what they have between them."

Patrolman Hooper listened, "You guys got someone in the back seat?"

Howard and Ben together answered no.

"You guys sure?"

"Why don't you check that back seat?" George suggested.

Patrolman Hooper asked Ben, "You a ventriloquist or something?"

"No, sir, I am not." Ben had lived in the South long enough to know when to place a good *sir*.

"How can you talk like that?" the policeman asked.

"I can't, sir," Ben answered. "That is George speaking."

Hooper looked at the names he had taken down and saw HOWARD and BENJAMIN. He read again, the ink on his bottom lip shifting from period to comma as he formed the words, HOWARD CARR and BENJAMIN CARR. "Is George one of you guy's middle names?" he asked.

George answered, "You might say that I am more of a middle man."

Ben smiled at Howard, "Yeah, you might say that. It's good having George back."

"Back?" Patrolman Hooper asked, "back seat?" he suggested further.

George said, "Why don't you let George speak for himself?"

And Patrolman Hooper said, "Yeah, why don't you guys let George speak for himself."

George did. He said, "Officer, I suggest that you search the back seat of that car. After you have done that, I think you would like to call the mother of these young men. Dial 798-4651 in this area code. You'll have to let it ring a long time. She sleeps very soundly."

The cop nodded and led them to the patrol car where he locked them in while he examined the back seat of the old blue Buick.

"Are you trying to get even with me, George?" Ben asked.

"No, Ben, I'm surprised that you ask. I'm merely doing what you know should be done."

Ben nodded. "I just wanted to be sure that we're in this together. Some of the best things are just understood between us." He then turned to Howard and said, "You know, we forced you into this whole thing, Howie."

Howard answered, "If you say so, I won't fight you, Ben. It's never fair. It's always two against one."

Patrolman Hooper pulled their car to the side of the road, emptied the back seat and carried the contents to his car, locked the old Buick, returned to the patrol car, called headquarters and told them that he was bringing in the Carr boys. Howard and Ben smiled at each other when they heard that. Hooper then told headquarters to telephone Mrs. Carr and tell her to meet them at the Juvenile Court House. He was about to put down his microphone when he added, "Ring it a long time; she sleeps sound." Then, shooting an embarrassed glance into the back seat, Patrolman Hooper took contents and criminals to the police station.

eleven

B<small>EN AND HOWARD</small> (and George) sat on a bench to the side of the desk while Patrolman Hooper filed a report with the counselor. The counselor was tired. He, too, was working overtime; instead of leaving at 11:30, he was staying so that he could advise and help those of the college crowd who would be brought to him. It would be that way all week. After the policeman filed his report, Counselor Boggs talked to Ben. He asked him if he had ever taken drugs himself, and he wanted to know if Ben was aware of the seriousness of what he had done. Did Ben know that the manufacture, sale, and general use of LSD had become illegal in 1966? And did he know how dangerous it could be to his health? Ben said that he didn't know the details, but that he knew that it was wrong.

Howard asked, "Where do you suppose Mom is?"

Counselor Boggs asked Ben, "Do you realize what you

have done, inviting your brother along, involving such a young man in traffic with drugs?

Ben said, "I don't mean to be fresh, sir, but he was invited along just for the drive. For the driving, really."

Howard leaned against Ben and asked, "How do you figure that Mom will get here since she won't have the car?"

George answered, "She'll arrive with Mr. Berkowitz."

Howard yawned and mumbled, "Thanks, George."

The counselor looked puzzled for a minute, then glanced at the forms that had been filled out by Patrolman Hooper. Ben saw him look at their names and then look again at their names. He said cautiously, "You won't find George written down."

Counselor Boggs looked up from his papers, Ben drew in his breath, and then he knew that he would tell. "George, you see, is the little man who lives inside of me. He's the guy that Dr. Herrold, my psychiatrist doesn't believe in. Neither does Marilyn, nor my father. No one believes in George except me and Howard. Howard knows George."

Counselor Boggs listened as Ben explained. He asked a question now and then, and once he consulted the telephone directory for the correct spelling of Dr. L. Daniel Herrold, practice limited to psychiatry. He realized that Ben was not a smart aleck trouble maker, and he realized that Howard was merely a sleepy little boy who had been brought along for the drive, for the driving.

(*143*)

Ben and Howard and George were sent to a small room to wait. The room was called Hold Room #2 and more than anything else, it resembled a bare, walk-in refrigerator with only one shelf. The shelf was a bench. Ben allowed his brother to lie across it while he sat on the floor and waited for his mother. She would arrive with Mr. Berkowitz. George would be proven correct. George knew so much; Ben was delighted to have him back and have him on his side.

Howard didn't want to sleep, but being horizontal, he was left with no choice. Ben saw his brother's eyes close; they seemed to lift the corners of his brother's mouth.

"What are you thinking about, Howie?" Ben asked.

"Only that they're going to have one heck of a time fingerprinting George."

Ben smiled and said, "They won't fingerprint George."

Howard answered sleepily, "You better believe they won't."

"And they won't fingerprint us either. We're underage. William isn't; he's seventeen already, and he can be tried as an adult in Florida. That's why George and I are taking the blame. That way it won't come to court and get the school and Mr. Berkowitz in trouble. It's never going to get in the papers even. Everyone thinks that I'm crazy anyway."

Howard yawned, "How nice," he said. His smile drooped; his jaw dropped. Howard always did sleep with his mouth open. Adenoids.

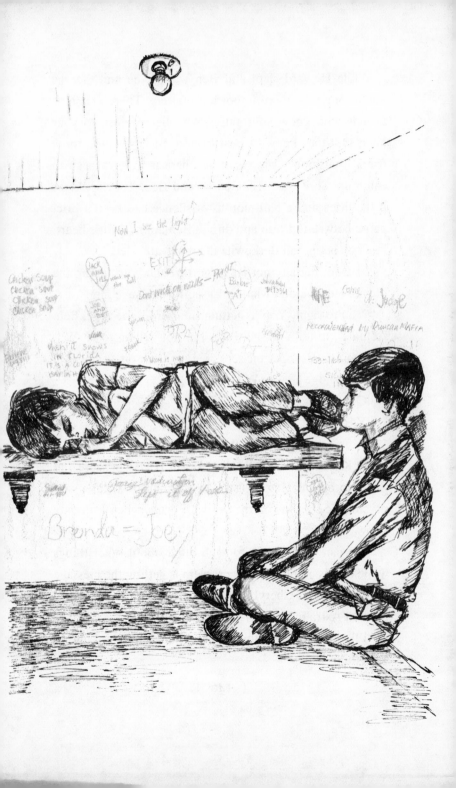

While Howard slept and Ben waited, he and George had a long talk about important matters. There are some friends who know your pulse, who lie so close to your heart that they know its beat from age to age. With those friends, cushioned always close, there is never a need to catch up. So it was with George and Ben. They spoke as if the three and a half months of silence had been a brief pause between the lub and dup of Benjamin's gentle heart.

"You better tell Berkowitz the real truth, Ben."

"If I do, he may not let us go through with taking the blame. He wouldn't want us to sacrifice to save him."

"You're right. You're getting smarter all the time, Ben. Actually, to tell you the truth, I'm not willing to let William and Cheryl get off scot free, and it isn't because of my old grudge against William."

"George?"

"Yes, Ben?"

"Admit that it is partly that. Partly your old grudge."

"O.K., Ben, it is partly that. But it is also because I'm going to hate having to listen to a bunch of lectures and psychiatric sessions on the perils of drugs when I already know them."

"We can silently talk to each other about other things while that is going on. The problem is getting the message to William and Cheryl without getting the research program at Astra in trouble?"

"I'll think of something, Ben. I'll enjoy thinking of something."

In the time between arrest and release, in the time that Howard slept, Ben and George completed their plans. George, Ben's little man, whom no one believed in, would get the blame. Everyone, legal, educational, and psychological, who would come to learn of the case, would believe that crazy Ben had attempted to manufacture and sell LSD to the college crowd. Because Ben was young and Ben was not normal, they would keep things quiet and private and not blame the whole school for one poor, sick, little boy's misconduct. When they would ask him about how he managed to get the stuff, he would tell them to ask George, and of course, George wouldn't tell.

Ben would have to continue seeing Dr. Herrold, but the authorities would consider Ben's age and the fact that he was under psychiatric care and would release him to his mother's custody. They would think that he, Ben, was not responsible for his actions; they would think that—even though Ben's sense of responsibility went farther and deeper than that of any normal boy.

Ben's chief worry was that the judge of the divorce court might find out and consider Mrs. Charlotte Carr an unfit mother. Ben realized that motherhood is the only profession where a person is not judged by the quality of the product. Everyone thought that Mrs. Hazlitt was one terrific mama, because she tried hard. They might want Ben to live with his father, but something (or was it George?) told Ben that Marilyn would think twice before taking Ben and Howard to live with her for all time. She would want the court to give Charlotte Carr another chance. And then another. Perhaps, divorce court would tell Mrs. Charlotte Carr that Ben needed the attentions of a father. Mr. Berkowitz would do for that.

"What are we going to do about William and Cheryl after all?" Ben asked.

"We're not going to do anything. We'll let Berkowitz do it. After all the fuss has calmed down, after Easter recess, after it's too late to change things but not before the end of school, we'll let Berkowitz do what must be done."

"What is that, George?"

"Give William and Cheryl failing grades for the rest of the year. Both of them. *F*'s for the whole course."

Ben laughed out loud. He knew that George had discovered the way. Bad grades were probably the only thing that would cause trouble for William and Cheryl at home. They would be asked for an explanation. They would tell the truth, maybe, and then their parents would investigate. Or they would lie, (probably!) and then their parents would march to the school to find out why it is possible for a teacher to fail them for an entire year on the basis of only part of the course—a voluntary part, at that. Mr. Berkowitz could take it from there. The truth would come out, and maybe their parents would even choose to do something about it.

Ben was grateful to George for taking the blame, and he told George so.

"It's all right, Ben; you don't have to grovel."

"I'm not grovelling; I am merely being polite. You can't recognize good manners because you don't have any yourself."

"That's right, I don't. I don't need them because I don't face the world. You shouldn't have manners with me, nor I with you. So I am not going to tell you, 'Don't mention it,' about the favor I am doing for you."

"If you're not going to say 'Don't mention it,' what are you going to say?"

"I'm going to say that you damn well should be grateful, and I'm going to ask a favor in return."

"Which is?"

"Which is to listen to me always—don't neglect me, Ben. Remember me now, especially now, as the pull of your courses and the pull of your classmates tries to drown out my voice forever. It's a critical time, Ben. Always listen to me, Ben. If you don't shut me up forever now, I'll be rich within you. You'll always have me to fall back on."

"O.K., George, I'll promise, but I don't really see how I can help but listen if you're talking."

"You can stop hearing me, Ben. Don't ever do that."

"I won't, George. You don't have to grovel."

Ben was resting on the floor, and Howard was sleeping when Mrs. Carr and Mr. Berkowitz arrived. Mr. Berkowitz's hair and moustache looked like a molting bird. He had buttoned his shirt wrong and had only one front flap tucked inside his pants. Mrs. Carr looked no better.

Ben told his mother that she would now have to *believe in* him in public and *believe* only what he would tell her in private. Charlotte Carr did that. She listened to what her son said in public and believed what he said in private.

And Mr. Berkowitz, hearing of Benjamin's troubles, waited for the real explanation to come along. When it did, after the court records had been made, after Ben was committed to his mother's care, after Ben was again under treatment at the psychiatrist's, after school had resumed, when the real explanation came, Mr. Berkowitz said thank you. He said thank you to Benjamin Dickinson Carr for wanting to help him, and he said thank you to Charlotte Carr for rearing him as she had. Mr. Berkowitz urged Ben to return to court and tell the truth. He would back him up, but Ben refused. He asked only that Cheryl and William get failing grades. That turned out to be the least and the most that he could do.

after

In the two years since these happenings, William and Cheryl have entered college. William did not get a scholarship that he was counting on because of his failing grade in chemistry and because of the poor recommendation written by Mr. Berkowitz. William is working part time in the college library to help pay for what the scholarship would have. He often feels very sorry for himself, and he hates Berkowitz and Ben. Hate is a hole; it can be filled, and maybe someday, it will be. With gratitude.

Cheryl is engaged to marry someone other than William. The whole incident left her slightly saddened and inconvenienced. Her parents took away her driving privileges until the following September.

Charlotte Carr became Mrs. Sheldon Berkowitz, and Howard is considering changing his name to Howard Berkowitz Carr instead of Howard Ferrari Carr. He watches his stepfather trim his moustache twice a week.

Yes, and Ben.

Ben was dismissed from the psychiatrist's care a year and a half after these happenings. Ben's own voice had deepened by then, and it had become indistinguishable from George's. But for all the rest of his life, Ben will be mindful of his inner parts. He'll watch his diet and never swallow orange seeds or watermelon pits because to do so could bring on an attack of appendicitis, and that he realizes would involve surgery.